Talisman

Talisman
Paul Murdoch

Published by Strident Publishing
© Sam Wilding 2015

Printed in the United Kingdom
Cover illustration and design © Ida Henrich

ISBN: 978-1-905537-66-2

James Peck, the lead character of the Denthan series, has asthma. For help and advice with asthma, please visit www.asthma.org.uk

Typeset in Lucida by Andrew Forteath. Printed by CPI Antony Rowe

The publisher acknowledges support from publication towards the ...

About Paul Murdoch

Born in Helensburgh, Scotland, Paul Murdoch grew up beside Loch Lomond, on the very edge of the Scottish Highlands. He studied Zoology at Glasgow University and has always maintained a strong interest in nature and the outdoors. He worked in wildlife reserves for a few years before becoming involved in the sales and marketing side of agriculture.

Always possessing a strong creative streak, Paul played rock guitar on tour in the UK, Holland and America, writing many songs along the way. He then put his talents to use in poetry and short stories, before penning *Talisman*.

Paul is also the author of the acclaimed eco-thriller, *Windscape* (written under pen-name Sam Wilding) – an adventure novel for young people that impartially explores the controversial topic of wind farms – and a series of picture books for younger children.

Home for Paul is still near Loch Lomond, an easy spot from which to reach the many schools he visits each year.

Acknowledgements

A huge thanks goes out to Greg Addison, Erin Crombie, Alan Sneddon, Billy Scobie, John O'Hare, Allyson and her boys, Traci in Arizona and to Kristina in New England. Also, a massive 'hats off' to Keith Charters for his final tweaks. But most of all, to my constant reality check and long-suffering wife, Katrina – who is not, by the way, the real 'Cathy'. Ah...hum...

This book was written in the wee small hours for my eldest boy, Ryan, but it was also inspired by, and is equally dedicated to his sisters and brother: Emma, Ruth, and Joe.

Love you all

1

The Footprint

High on Bruce Moor, James ran over the rough ground towards the ancient circle of stones known to the locals as the Jesus Rocks. This random collection of standing stones cast an eerie imprint on an otherwise flawless blue sky.

The base of each stone was covered in damp green moss that glistened in the sunlight, while the tops were a confection of rust-coloured lichens and flaking algae.

The familiar white graffiti was still daubed on the tallest stone. He could just about make out 'JESUS SAVES'. The letters had begun to fade, which added to James's feeling of sadness.

He plonked himself down on a springy tussock of heather and gazed out over the loch below. Although the sky was clear and the weather warm, the loch's dark waters filled him with foreboding.

Why had his dad had left home without saying goodbye? There'd been no explanation, not even a note or an apologetic mumble on the answering machine. All of his dad's clothes were still folded in his cupboard and his cherished bird books remained undisturbed on their dusty shelves.

Quickly wiping away the tear that rolled down his cheek, James tried to imagine what his dad might have said if he'd actually taken the time to say goodbye.

"It's like this, Son – I've really enjoyed knowing you for the last ten years, but I have to go away for a while. I'll be back to go bird-watching and bike rides, and I'll even take

mum and yourself somewhere exciting, like Ardrossan or maybe Spain. So don't worry. Okay?"

His dad's deep, reassuring voice still rattled around in James's head, and he wondered how long it would take before he forgot how it sounded.

It upset him when his mum refused to talk about his dad's disappearance. She couldn't even say his name without throwing something or shouting. So James had given up. He didn't need the hassle. He just didn't mention it any more. Not to her.

It didn't make sense to him. His dad had vanished, yet nobody was doing anything about it. There were no search parties, no 'missing dad' posters, nothing on the T.V., just embarrassing gossip in the local paper that said things like *'Drumfintley Scout leader, David Peck has, in wife's words, "done a runner"'.*

So, he thought, *Mum is happy to talk to the press about Dad, but not me.*

Everyone in Drumfintley knew his mum was fiery and unpredictable. Even a little scary. She said exactly what she thought without a care for the consequences.

His dad, on the other hand, was the opposite – reliable, safe...normal. Even pretty boring at times; but in a nice sort of way. *'Doing a runner'* was completely out of character.

Frustrated, James picked up a smooth, rust-coloured pebble and launched it as hard as he could against the largest of the standing stones. His dad *hadn't* run off. James knew in his heart that something bad had happened. That was why he'd climbed all the way up to Bruce Moor. This was the last place his dad had been seen, and James was determined to find some kind of clue that would prove everyone wrong.

After a puff of his inhaler and another stretched-out sigh, he blinked and refocused. There, beside the pebble he'd thrown a moment before, a little animal lay dead.

Crushed flat, its eyes bulged out of its furry brown head like two tiny, black marbles. The poor wee thing's legs were splayed and pressed deep into the soft peat.

Stretching forward to grab a clump of heather, James stood up and moved a little closer. It looked as though the creature had been killed mid-pounce.

Squinting down at the flattened pelt, James took a moment to try and work out if the dead animal was a stoat or a weasel. One had a long, bushy tail, while the other only possessed a small stumpy one…

It was then, as he was trying to recall which had the bigger tail, that he noticed the footprint.

The cause of the little creature's demise was now clear. It had been stamped on, squashed flat. *But by what? What kind of creature can move fast enough to do such a thing?* Stranger still, judging by the mark on the ground, whatever had made the print had been barefoot. James could still see the indentations made by its long, skinny toes. He counted them under his breath. "One, two, three… only three."

He placed his own foot beside the print for comparison, revealing the footprint to be at least four times longer than his, even without counting the three spindly toes.

Moving further into the Jesus Rocks, James scanned the ground for any other matching prints.

While there were signs that the beast had moved away from the stones, he saw no trace of it inside the circle.

Ruling out that it could be a prank, James ran a hand through his short, mousy brown hair and considered the other possibilities. He remembered that, apart from his dad's disappearance, the local paper had recently run a series of stories about 'big cats'. James had read this with great interest.

It turned out that some very stupid people had once kept panthers and lions as pets, but had let them go. The government had decided to make them pay extra taxes for keeping them, so they'd simply set them loose. *A big cat would be fast enough to do this kind of thing, but what about those long, spindly toes?*

The paper had gone on to say that only recently Mrs Galdinie, who owned the sweetshop, had seen a tiger prowling amongst the bins at the back of her house. The paper had also said that Mr Mullet, the shepherd from Glenhead Farm, was convinced that some kind of animal was responsible for his missing sheep.

Unnerved by the thought of a huge cat prowling the moor, James began to panic. Would it attack a ten-year-old boy? *Of course it would. Ten-year-old boys are probably its favourite kind of food, next to bin spillings and raw sheep.*

Looking round, he wondered if the creature might still be on the moor, crouching and watching him. There were plenty of gorse bushes and rocks it could be hiding behind, poised to attack, waiting for him to stray within striking distance.

He edged back into the stone circle.

Strangely, the further he moved from the trampled animal, the more uneasy he became. He was alone amongst the crooked stones, and far above the safety of the village below.

He became aware of a change on the moor: the curlew's trilling song faded; one by one, the skylarks fluttered down from the sky, silent, as if shot by some unseen hunter. Before long, the only thing he could hear was the rustle of the heather at his feet, but then that stopped too. It was as if someone had pressed a magical remote control and put the whole world on pause.

There was silence. Complete and utter silence. Too terrified to make a sound, he held his breath. But unable to keep this up for long, he took a gulp of air, choked and then practically erupted. A whole string of very loud coughs and splutters echoed over the moor. When he stopped, all he could hear was his own laboured breathing growing louder and louder. His wheezing took on an eerie, unearthly tone that soon became unbearable. Goosebumps sprouted on his bare legs and a cold shiver tickled the base of his spine.

He had the uncomfortable feeling that someone or something was watching him.

"Brilliant," he whispered to himself, "some three-toed cat-monster is going to attack, and there's nobody around to save me."

He convinced himself he would die alone and in agony. He pictured his dad pinned to the ground, helpless and seconds from death; now *he* was going to disappear, too. He could imagine the Drumfintley Herald headline: *Giant killer feline slaughters father...then eats son for dessert.*

James steadied himself against one of the standing stones as the feeling of impending doom made his muscles tense and his neck damp with sweat.

The unbearable silence seemed to close in on him. There was a very low rumbling. The ground beneath him began to shake.

Screaming, James bolted out of the Jesus Rocks and raced across the moor. He ran as fast as he could, onto the path and down through the dark woods without so much as a backwards glance. Unseen branches clawed at his hair and whipped his skinny, bare legs.

Half running, half stumbling, he skidded over the rocky farm track until, breathless and blinded by sweat, he reached the underpass.

2

The Stranger

James stopped inside a corrugated tunnel and steadied himself on the cold, steel wall. Fighting for every lungful of air, he fumbled for his inhaler and eagerly sucked in the snowy white mist. A horrible sensation of drowning had built in his chest, but within seconds it began to ease.

Coughing out the majority of the mist, and still panting, he staggered on through the tunnel until he could see the familiar, moss-covered rooftops of Drumfintley.

He'd let a wretched bag of trampled fur freak him out. And he'd run off like a maniac and nearly triggered an asthma attack into the bargain. He shuddered at the thought of having an asthma attack while he was alone, out on the moor. *Just as lethal as being mauled to death by a big cat,* he thought, *and a lot more likely.*

He took a shaky breath and felt the blood rush to his cheeks.

The familiar noise of cars and lorries roaring along the bypass overhead brought him back to reality. Even the underpass smell of stale wine and wee made him feel better.

Breathing more easily, he headed down to the village shop on Main Street. The store stocked a good selection of wildlife books for the odd tourist who stumbled into the village, usually by mistake. There was a good chance of finding a picture of a weasel or a stoat in one of those. And he needed *something* to take his mind off the feeling of dread that had engulfed him on the moor.

Not wanting to attract the attention of the

gossipmongers, James sneaked into the store behind the Italian sweetshop owner Mrs Galdinie and hunkered down, out of sight. He rummaged, unseen, amongst a muddle of magazines and books before pausing to listen.

He could hear the unmistakable voice of the village drunk, Gauser — a stout, scruffy man who held his trousers up with orange twine and sported a moth-eaten soldier's jacket that stank of stale booze. "No doubt about it," growled Gauser in an affected Irish lilt, "Cathy Peck has the temperament of a killer, so she has."

"Rubbish!" Mrs Galdinie exclaimed.

On hearing his mum's name, James made a small space between the magazines and peered through. He could see Mrs Galdinie's appalled expression and smiled to himself as she bristled to his mum's defence. "There's nothing wrong with Cathy Peck!" she announced.

Gauser placed another pack of square sausage on the counter and nodded his head. "No dat's right. Nothing that a twenty year stretch in the nick couldn't fix."

He turned his back on Mrs Galdinie and addressed the checkout girl.

"Ever seen the Peck woman on one of her rants?" Gauser slurred 'rants', and then steadied himself against the till.

The skinny checkout girl giggled and leaned forward. She spoke softly. "Of course. Wait until I tell you this one…"

Gauser screwed his face up into a toothless grin as he spun round to face Mrs Galdinie. "See!"

The girl began. "Cathy Peck came in last Christmas for some custard." She drummed her fingers on the till. "Anyway, she had her son and that poor husband of hers with her. Well, for reasons best known to herself, Mrs Peck began shouting. Went for her man there and then, like some deranged tiger."

James twitched at the mention of the word 'tiger'.

The checkout girl gave Gauser a swift nod. "That boy of hers was *so* embarrassed." She took Gauser's money and handed him back his change. But the Irishman wasn't ready to leave.

Mrs Galdinie fidgeted impatiently in the queue behind him.

The checkout girl continued. "After screaming at him like a maniac, Cathy Peck actually grabbed her man by the throat. When her son asked her to calm down, she clattered *him* across the ear and then barged out of the shop."

James rubbed his left ear as he recalled the clout.

Gauser moved closer and assumed a pirate-like tone, his voice husky and gravelly. "The throat, you said?"

The checkout girl looked confused. "Well, I think it was…"

"You said the Peck woman grabbed her man by the throat, didn't ye?" Gauser persisted.

The checkout assistant nodded, looking unsure of herself.

"Now, dat's where you're off the mark," roared Gauser. The deep wrinkles on his ruddy face shifted to form a smug expression. "David Peck wasn't strangled." He moved his puffed up lips close to the girl's ear and, in a whisper laced with spit, said, "He was poisoned."

The 'p' of 'poison' was to blame for a big dousing of phlegm.

"Poisoned!" she yelped, furiously wiping her ear with the edge of her sleeve.

The checkout girl's startled expression had caused several other shoppers to shop a little closer.

James watched as Mrs Galdinie, losing patience, pushed Gauser aside. While holding her nose, she handed the checkout girl the exact amount for a tub of double cream and shook her head. "Estupido!" she scolded nasally. "What about di big cat at my bins, eh? And why did di polis arrest old Archie MacNulty then?"

Gauser waved Mrs Galdinie and her suggestions away with a terse flick of his thick, dirty fingers. "Away with ye. Der's no big cats around here." He paused, pulling on the twine that held up his trousers. "As fir MacNulty, well, he was just di last person to see him alive, dat's all. MacNulty's always up on the moor poachin' wi' his ferrets."

"You are a rude man," said Mrs Galdinie, her pencilled brows scrunching into a petulant frown.

As she made for the door, six other shoppers looked away, needlessly busying themselves to avoid her gaze. She was well known for putting a hex on people or, worse, banning them from her sweet shop. She sold the best homemade tablet in the world, and the tastiest ice cream.

Nobody had noticed James flicking through the wildlife books, which had revealed that the squashed animal had been a stoat. And now, kneeling behind the wall of crisps, comics and magazines, he didn't dare move. His only thought was how he might escape from the shop unseen, before people became overcome with embarrassment and apologised, or pretended they were talking about something other than his mum and dad.

He couldn't believe that the villagers thought his mum was a murderer. It was bad enough that they thought his dad had deserted them. James felt nauseous.

The shop door had just swung shut behind Mrs Galdinie when the bell pinged.

A newcomer's massive frame loomed over the till and everyone stopped flustering and gossiping.

James, still clutching the wildlife book, looked down at the stranger's feet. There were no spindly toes, but the stranger himself was a bit of an oddity. He was so tall that his head had clipped some of the dangly advertising boards that swung from the ceiling. In his left hand was a large, gnarled stick. His clothes were old-fashioned, even frumpy, and made of a material James had never seen before. Long, black hair fell over his broad shoulders, giving him the appearance of an eccentric hippy or a rock musician.

The stranger's voice was exceptionally deep. "Good day," he said. "Could someone point me in the direction of Drumfintley Park?"

Those in the shop looked at each other, wondering who would answer first. Suspicious of anyone who kept their sunglasses on inside, they hesitated.

James stood up. "I can help."

The whole shop, with the exception of the stranger, gasped at seeing James Peck emerge from behind the comic rack. But James knew this was the only way to leave with some sense of purpose and pride. He placed his book back on the shelf. "I can take you there if you like," he offered. He struggled to stifle a building asthmatic cough, which threatened to sputter and hiss from his lips as he moved closer to the door.

"Thank you, but a few pointers will suffice," said the stranger.

James wasn't sure what 'suffice' meant, but he took his chance and stepped out onto the pavement with a huge sigh of relief, glad to be free of the shoppers' stares and mutterings.

The stranger followed, then stopped for a moment to take in the warm Drumfintley air before scratching at his temple irritably for a few seconds and staring down at James.

"It's not far," James reassured, squinting against the glaring sunlight. "You see the church spire?" He pointed towards St. Donan's.

"Indeed, I do," replied the stranger, moving past him.

"Well," James shouted after him, "when you get as far as the church, turn right and you'll see the park."

"Thank you, and many felicitations to you, my boy," the stranger replied.

'Felicitations'? James raised his hand to wave, but the stranger didn't look back.

James watched the tall stranger for a few moments. His mannerisms were...unusual. He moved with a strange deliberation, stopping every so often to sniff the air, like a wild animal.

Curious, James decided to follow him.

3

A Chance Meeting

James wished that his best friend Craig was there for some support. But if he doubled back for his pal now he might lose track of the stranger.

No, he could do this by himself. He would just have to make sure he kept well out of sight.

Besides, anything was better than listening to those doom-merchants back in the shop.

James followed as the stranger turned down Park Street. After a few seconds, however, he had to duck behind a lamppost. The stranger had skidded to a stop, his long, black hair fanning out as he glanced back up the street.

James froze, and waited until he heard the clicking of the stranger's stick against the tarmac again before he looked out. Ahead, the tall eccentric was moving on towards the rusting, wrought-iron gates that marked the entrance to Drumfintley Park.

The stick, James decided, was not for support. The stranger walked briskly, in long strides. It was a struggle to keep up with him.

Once in the park, James darted off the main path and slipped into the bushes. He moved amongst an assortment of chip pokes and empty beer cans. The park was always a dump after the spring fair.

Deflated, James reasoned that the stranger was probably one of the people from the fair who'd left something behind and had returned to find it. But if so, why would he need directions to the park?

A horrible scream interrupted James's train of thought. "Arghh!"

In his efforts to hide himself in the rhododendron bushes, James had lost sight of the stranger, but he was sure the scream had come from the direction of the old bandstand. He crouched low and crawled through the dead leaves until he could just see the back of the stranger's head.

James tensed as the stranger spoke. "I'm too busy for this nonsense, understand? You've had plenty of time!" The stranger thumped his gnarled stick into something soft and another yelp echoed through the trees. "I have to finish things in Denthan. So, can I rely on you to find and kill him? I mean, it's not as though he's capable of performing any magic in his present form, is it? All you have to do is step on him and that will be that."

Unbidden, a pulse flicked in James's neck. He checked for his inhaler, but paused to listen as a second voice echoed up from below.

"Listensss ssssire... Upsss there, in the bushessss... Did you hear thatsssss?"

James ducked down, praying that his cough would stay trapped in his chest.

"I thought I heard somethssss..."

But before the hissing voice could finish, the gnarled stick found its mark once more.

"Argh! Ssstop hurting. Pleasssss..."

James had never heard a voice quite like this one before. An evil hissing overlapped every syllable. He covered his mouth and coughed through his fingers.

The stranger's voice masked his spluttering. "It's only your underdeveloped imagination, Sleven. Now, can you kill him or not?"

"Yes, yes, yesssss..."

Watery eyed, James wondered who this Sleven had

been instructed to kill. He edged forward, then slowly raised himself onto his elbows. Lifting his head an inch at a time, he reached a point where he could just see inside the old bandstand.

To his alarm, it was now completely deserted.

Where have they gone? James banged his head on a branch and then shuffled back through the bushes the same way he'd come in. Soaked through with sweat, and short of breath, he saw the park gates up ahead. Tall and ominous, they loomed over the flowerbeds and litter-strewn lawns. Glancing between the exit and the bushes behind him, he tried to decide whether he should make a run for the gates or walk out nonchalantly as if nothing terrifying had happened.

He had just decided on the slow walk when a voice filled his head.

"About time, too," it said.

James threw himself to the ground behind the nearest black council bin.

This was a different voice from the ones he'd heard at the bandstand.

"Quickly now. Get me out of here," it said.

This voice was rich, like an actor's, but impatient. To James's horror, it seemed to be only inches away. He peered over the edge of the bin, only to pull back with a scream as a wasp flew out of a lemonade can.

"Yes, that's right, I'm in the bin. Look again!" ordered the voice.

This time, James eased himself up onto his knees and peered inside. There, behind an orange nappy sack and a pile of half-eaten chicken-fried-rice, something moved. It flashed gold, then orange and yellow in the sunlight. Still scanning the park for danger, James picked up a twig and pushed the nappy sack to the side. Underneath, he saw a clear plastic bag half filled with water. Inside, a little goldfish peered straight up at him.

Looking about nervously, he lifted the bag from the rubbish and slumped back down behind the bin. He prodded it gently to see if the fish was still alive.

"Stop that!" scolded the voice. "There's no time to waste. You have to get us out of here!"

James blinked and held the goldfish closer to his face. He was definitely losing his mind. He looked round the side of the bin, but there was no one there. "It can't be the fish," he whispered.

"Yes it can," said the voice. "My name is Mendel."

James dropped the plastic bag and pushed himself away from it, kicking backwards across the grass as he balanced on his elbows.

He'd seen the fish's lips move.

"I... I don't think I'm feeling too well," James groaned.

"You look healthy enough to me," remarked the voice. "However, I don't rate your chances of remaining that way if we stay here much longer."

James couldn't believe what he was hearing. The voice in his head was as clear as any hi-fi, and yet the only possible source was the goldfish.

Then, to James's horror, the bushes behind him rustled loudly. A branch snapped and a fat wood-pigeon broke cover above his head.

He scrambled back onto the path that led to the exit, but the bag with the goldfish was still on the grass beside the bin. Something inside was telling him to leave it there, but he couldn't, so he dashed back and snatched it up before sprinting for the park gates.

"Not so fast, please! You're making me feel quite sick." The voice rattled round in James's head as he ran up Park Street, but he was too busy trying to get as far away as he could from whatever had startled the wood-pigeon to pay much attention to what it was saying.

As he turned the corner onto Main Street, he chanced a look behind him and glimpsed a bald, lanky man in the rhododendron bushes back in the park. The heavy black bin, where he'd found the goldfish, now lay overturned, its muck and filth scattered all over the path.

"Sleven will not follow us in daylight." The voice in his head almost caused James to trip up.

"What... who is Sleven?" James felt a bit stupid talking down at the little fish.

"Sleven is the least of our worries."

"*Our* worries?" said James. *Why didn't I just leave the goldfish beside the bin?*

"Look, I think it would be best if you just got me back to your house as quickly and as smoothly as possible, James." The voice had adopted a more friendly tone.

"How do you know my name?" James felt his mouth become dry and he was beginning to grow short of breath again.

"Try to remain calm," said the voice, "I will explain everything once we're safe."

As James ran up past the village hall and into Willow Terrace, he tried not to think about his mum's likely reaction on seeing the goldfish. She had a stringent anti-pets policy.

Growing more frightened with every step, he bounded past the Fyffe's car and raced up his garden path. He pushed open the door, clambered inside, and slammed it shut. After slipping the bolt, he placed the bulging plastic bag on the first step of the wooden staircase.

Staring at the tiny goldfish swimming around inside, James's head reeled with images of the longhaired stranger and the blood-curdling voice of Sleven. He had a feeling that these people were involved in his dad's disappearance. He didn't know how or why exactly, but he was convinced that they were, and it frightened him.

He pinched his arm just to make sure he wasn't dreaming.

But he wasn't, because it stung like mad.

4

The Wizard Goldfish

After rummaging about at the back of their garage, James had found an old tin bath, a bit bashed and a little rusty, but just right for the job. He had hauled it up to his bedroom and filled it with tap water from the bathroom.

From time to time, a horrible feeling of dread would wash over him and he'd peer out the window, half expecting to see the longhaired stranger – or perhaps his deranged, hissing accomplice – walking up the garden path. He shuddered at the thought of those two ne'er-do-wells somehow being involved in his dad's disappearance.

He should have gone straight to the Police, but there was the small matter of the talking fish to consider.

"I could do with some fresh water, please," said the voice.

James turned round to look at the goldfish on his bedside table. "Are you really talking to me?"

"Yes, I am," said the fish. "And can I also remind you that my name is Mendel?" The fish named Mendel pushed a big, golden, googly eye against the bulging plastic bag. "Needless to say, I've ended up in my present form by ill fate rather than by design."

"You mean you're not normally a goldfish?" asked James.

"That would be correct," said Mendel, his tone slightly reproachful. "Fresh water?" he prompted.

"Oh, yes, of course." James held the bag over the old tin bath and undid the knot that kept Mendel inside his little fairground prison. "There you go!"

Mendel slipped into the bath and sighed with relief. "Three weeks in a plastic bag. I thought I was going to die in there. How can your race be so cruel to their fellow creatures?"

"My race?" said James. "You mean you're not from Drumfintley?"

"Not exactly," Mendel answered, sounding excited as he darted around his new home.

"We used to have a goldfish," said James, changing the subject, "but the cat smashed the bowl and..." James thought back to the cat licking its lips after its fishy snack and wished he hadn't begun the story. "Anyway, I'm sure we've got some grit and stuff somewhere."

He pulled his chair across the floor and placed it beneath the wardrobe. Then, standing on his tiptoes, he fumbled around amongst the boxed games and piles of magazines. "Ah! Here they are." He lifted down a small carrier bag and pulled out the various bits and pieces. With a sense of self-satisfaction, he smiled at Mendel and tipped a heap of blue and orange gravel into the water. Then, after spreading the little stones round the bath, he dropped in a plastic castle followed by three clumps of fake seaweed.

Satisfied with his handiwork, he took one more look out of his bedroom window.

"The people in the park were looking for you, weren't they?" said James.

"Indeed, they were. But you came along, just as I predicted."

"Predicted?" asked James.

"Chance and science are interlinked, my boy. Quite fascinating if you do the right calculations." Mendel became serious. "Sleven will still try to kill me tonight."

"Why?" James paced his room, nervously twirling his blue inhaler.

"Because he would not dare fail his master." Ominously Mendel added: "Unless you help me, he will succeed."

James bounced back down onto the bed. "I've already helped you. What am I supposed to do now?" His stomach tightened as he thought of what he'd got himself into. He wouldn't be in this mess if he'd stood up earlier and endured the shoppers' stares. If only he hadn't followed the stranger. If only his dad had waited home that night instead of traipsing up the hill to avoid his mum's bad mood.

If, if, if.

Becoming more morose by the second, James noticed the blue and white neckerchiefs dangling from his wall. Pinned there by his dad, the Drumfintley Scouts' colours reminded him of the time he'd won the orienteering competition. A little plaque said:

> *1st prize*
> *James Peck*
> *5th Drumfintley Scout Group*

That had been a year ago, when everything had been normal.

"Mendel?" James approached the tin bath intending to ask the question most important to him, the question that had burned in his mind night and day for three weeks. He cleared his throat. "It's about my dad. Do you know where—?"

"I'm sorry, James. I don't think I can help you with that. Not yet."

"But I haven't finished!" James gasped. "I mean, I haven't asked you what I want to ask you!"

Mendel replied calmly, "It's what people don't say that

reveals their innermost thoughts. But I really must insist you come a little closer." Mendel's voice had a sleepy ring to it. James knelt beside the tin bath, seething in silence. He could still see the goldfish down amongst the fake weed, flicking its fins, pulsating.

"I need you to help me," said Mendel, "and to do this properly I need you to touch my scales."

James drew back a little. "What?"

"Just put your hand into the water," whispered Mendel.

As soon as the words came into his mind, James felt an incredible urge to put his hand into the bath. He flinched when his fingers broke the surface tension of the water. Every molecule brushed against his skin. Like a million tiny needles, the cool liquid jabbed and soothed at the same time.

Slowly, the cuff of his shirt disappeared beneath the surface...

"Aagghh!" James yelled as his forefinger brushed against the golden scales, electricity shooting up his arm and forking down into his heart. An incredible tightness gripped him. He panted, trying to catch his breath.

"Don't move," ordered Mendel. "Just remain still for a minute or two. I'm sorry about the pain, but if I had explained the whole process, I doubt you would have helped."

James's eyes flashed open the moment his thoughts and memories returned to him. He kicked himself away from the bath. Every muscle in his body felt stiff and sore.

"W...what? You tricked me!"

"I said don't move." Mendel's voice echoed round in his mind. "I'm sorry, James, but you will soon see that by making this connection you have probably saved us both. Now sit up and look at me."

James pulled himself back over to the tub, intent on tipping the whole lot down the toilet, fish and all, when all of a sudden the water in the tin bath began to ripple. He felt a tickle in his throat, and then he muttered something that sounded like, "Wwwviswwinpoowwlww." Tears ran down his face, and a persistent knocking sensation thumped inside his head. Despite the pain, he almost laughed out loud at the ridiculous word that had spilled from his lips. It had sounded like someone talking underwater.

He gulped as the water in the tin bath turned blood red, then a deep, tropical blue.

"What are you doing?" James exclaimed, his throat suddenly dry. But there was no reply. Wisps of smoke spun on the surface of the water then cleared to reveal a familiar sight: the nine stone pillars that formed the Jesus Rocks. They were clearly visible on the surface of the water. Standing proud of the heather, they looked like the fingers of some long-forgotten giant that had been buried under the hill. Even the familiar graffiti marring the biggest stone couldn't stop him from feeling that he was seeing something for the first time.

"You are looking into a vision pool," explained Mendel.

"I was there this morning," said James, thinking back to the squashed stoat, the strange footprint, and the uncontrollable panic that had overwhelmed him.

"I know you were," said Mendel, "but there is something in the stone circle that may help us both." He paused. "You felt something there this morning, didn't you, James?"

"Yes. Well I... Are you a wizard or something?" pressed James.

"I prefer the word *scientist*, if you don't mind," Mendel replied. "Much less mysterious and wishy-washy. Don't you think?"

"I suppose." James gulped. "And my dad?"

"Your father's disappearance *may* be linked to the same dark magic that brought me here."

"It may?" gasped James.

"Yes," said Mendel. "And I *may* be able to help you if you can help me."

"Help you do what?" asked James, dreading the answer.

The vision pool's image of the Jesus Rocks became blurred until, with a sound like fat spitting in a hot pan, the water bubbled and then settled again. The picture now centred on the biggest stone.

"I need you to go back there right away. I need you to help me get back home," said Mendel.

5

Craig Harrison

James stared at the standing stone and wondered what Mendel meant by 'home'. More importantly, he wondered how his dad could possibly be involved in this whole weird scenario.

"James, you need to go back to that stone today. I need you to retrieve a blue crystal that lies at its base." The vision pool changed perspective, suddenly spiralling up and away from the main stone.

James felt sick. "But Sleven and the stranger," he began. "Was that Sleven's—?"

"—footprint that you saw up on the moor?" finished Mendel.

James hated it when Mendel delved into his thoughts. It felt like he was being robbed.

"I should think so," continued Mendel, answering his own question, "but don't worry. I've told you already. He won't brave your sun on a day like this. His body is covered in ink pustules that can burst in bright light. The more that burst, the less powerful his magic."

"Ink pustules?" said James, distractedly.

Just then the vision pool zoomed in on a patch of grass just beyond the body of the crushed stoat.

"James," said Mendel, "there is a blue crystal buried here that is crucial to our survival. It will take us back to my world. But that will only be the beginning. Once I'm back home we will need to find a talisman."

"A talisman?" whispered James.

"Yes," said Mendel. "Without the talisman I cannot

hope to save my world."

"What does the talisman look like?" asked James.

"I'm not sure," said Mendel, "but I am sure that your father was meant to disappear and that you and I were drawn together for a reason. As I said before, chance and science are interlinked. You will know what the talisman is when you hold it in your hands."

"I will?" said James, dreamily. "Look, I can't go off to some world to find a talis..."

"Talisman," said Mendel.

"Some mystery thingy," said James, becoming annoyed and panicky at the same time. "My mum won't let me."

"So, you would let a billion lifeforms die just because you're a bit scared of your mum?"

James laughed nervously. "A *bit* scared?"

"Unless you help me, everything – every*one* – on my planet will be incinerated. Mothers, brothers, sisters..." Mendel paused and then added, "...fathers."

The downstairs doorbell buzzed into life.

Annoyed by the interruption, James pushed himself up onto his feet. "Why can't you get the crystal yourself? Find the talisman. Just do some magic or—"

A familiar voice cut him short. "James!"

It was Craig, his best friend.

James shouted down through his open bedroom door. "How did you get in?"

Craig was already tramping up the stairs. "The front door was wide open, y' numpty!" he bellowed.

James was positive he'd pulled it shut. "It can't have been."

"It was open. Trust me," said Craig. He laughed his usual laugh, the one that began with a titter and ended in a guffaw. Tall for eleven, he had blond, spiky hair and a face full of freckles. Craig feigned a Scottish accent and said, "Ye cumin oot t' play?"

Catching Craig by the arm and leading him back down to the front door, James shook his head. "You know, it's really pathetic when you do the accent thing. You're from London, just accept it. Nobody's perfect."

James paused on the front steps and looked back up in the direction of his room. Relieved that he had shut his bedroom door behind him, he was just about to suggest they go up onto the moor when Craig said, "Fancy going up to the Jesus Rocks? I mean I know we've not played there for a while because... You know...? That's where your dad lost the plot and scarpered." Craig wasn't the most diplomatic boy in the world. He gave a big, toothy grin and was about to blurt out some other pearl of wisdom when James pulled him back into the hallway.

"What's wrong with your face?" blurted Craig.

A black Volkswagen had screeched to a halt at the front gate. They heard the clump of the car door and footsteps on the garden path.

"It's Mum," said James, in a sharp whisper.

"You mean the Wicked Witch of the West?" laughed Craig...a laugh cut short when a familiar voice said, "Witch? I'll witch you!" Cathy Peck narrowed her eyes at James, as if *he*'d said it.

James immediately pointed a finger at Craig, "It was him."

"Get yourselves outside! A dry day like this, and you two are in front of the telly growing fatter by the minute!"

Struggling with five carrier bags and a bunch of keys, she barged past Craig and grunted.

James tried to explain. "We weren't watching TV, Mum."

"Yeah, right," she snapped. "You're a born liar, just like your dad."

James stared at the floor, burning with embarrassment, annoyed by the way she'd spoken about his dad in front of Craig. "We'll get out of your way, Mum," he muttered.

"So you're just going to let me struggle with the rest of the shopping?" She sneered at them both before flicking a strand of long, black hair from her eyes and marching past them.

"Thanks for dropping me in it, *pal*," whispered Craig.

"What do you expect?" snapped James. "She's in one of her moods."

They followed her back out to the car.

James thought Craig would probably quite enjoy watching his mum struggle with the rest of her shopping bags, so he was quietly relieved when his best friend lifted a huge bottle of diluting juice from the kerb.

"That's right. Get your gormless friends to do all the work," snapped his mum. "And stop hunching over like that! No wonder you can't breathe!" James knew she hated the way he wheezed and spluttered all the time.

"Why can't you just leave it for once?" James whispered angrily.

Unfortunately his mum had very good hearing and a can of beans whizzed through the air, narrowly missing his head.

"Hey! What was that for?" James protested.

Cathy clenched her fists. "In! You're grounded for the rest of the day!"

"But..." James began to protest, "I need to..."

"One more word and I'll make it a week," she snapped.

When she'd disappeared into the house, James turned to Craig and pulled him close. "Look, can you go up to the Jesus Rocks by yourself?"

"In!" Cathy Peck's voice resounded from the kitchen as she thumped an assortment of straining bags onto the kitchen table.

James spoke as quickly as he could to his friend. "The biggest rock has a blue crystal buried at its base. It will be brilliant in Geography class on Monday. How about it,

Craig, will you go and get it?"

Craig stared at James in complete disbelief. "What are you on about? We don't have Geography on Monday, and what blue crystal is this?" He made the mistake of following James into the house.

"Out!" screeched Cathy. She picked up another can of beans and held it like a shot-putt.

Craig put his hands up, as if someone had just pulled a gun on him, and backed out the front door.

"In!" This time Cathy stared hard at James and thumped the can down on the kitchen table.

Just before Craig stepped outside, James ran to the front door and grabbed his sleeve, "Just go and get it! I'll explain everything tomorrow. Trust me. I need you to do this for me. It's a matter of life or death."

"Right!" Cathy Peck had caught hold of James's ear. "Get in now," she threatened, her face red with rage, "or I'll make it a month."

As soon as Cathy turned away from him, Craig mouthed 'Wicked Witch of the West', and nodded, as if there was nothing more certain in the whole world.

As James was dragged into the kitchen, he watched his best friend edge down the garden path. He wasn't sure Craig would go all the way up to Bruce Moor by himself – he was a lazy oaf at the best of times.

Craig, however, pointed in the direction of the moor and nodded.

* * *

After a long climb and almost an hour of searching the Jesus Rocks, Craig pulled hard on a piece of material he'd discovered at the base of the biggest stone. A glint of deep azure blue made him smile. He lifted the crystal free before sitting down in the heather. About the same size as his TV remote control, it was surprisingly heavy and incredibly beautiful. Craig held it up to the sun and screeched out in delight as a cascade of tiny white dots danced over his face.

* * *

Far away in Denthan, the tall stranger tensed. He made a fist with his left hand, then relaxed, letting his long, black hair fall over the back of his ivory throne. He closed his cat-like eyes and delved deep into the thoughts of Craig Harrison.

6

What a Racket

Magical shapes lit up the sky over James's house. But in Willow Terrace nobody noticed a thing, not even nosy Ephie Blake at number fifty-four, who lay snoring and muttering beneath a pile of discarded sweet wrappers.

In their baskets, all the dogs were safely curled up, twitching and snarling at imaginary cats, while all the real cats continued prowling the Terrace, oddly oblivious to the cold morning mist that danced over the Peck's house.

Sparks flew over the frosted slates and random flares of light traced the windowpanes. First blue and then a piercing yellow, the colours shot up into the morning sky, glowing brightly before forming candescent clouds of mist that swirled and shimmered in the early dawn.

For the entire night, James had lain awake on his bed, hoping beyond hope that there would be no signs of Sleven or the tall stranger, both of whom seemed intent on murder.

Mendel's rich voice had remained silent since the previous afternoon and James wondered if the little fish had taken umbrage at his failure to retrieve the blue crystal from the Jesus Rocks. It wasn't *his* fault; he'd been grounded. At any rate, he still doubted whether Craig would have trailed all the way up the hill on his own.

Suddenly, something flashed yellow outside the window.

"Did you see that?" James sat up, dragging his bedclothes over to the tin bath. "Mendel, wake up!"

The little goldfish didn't move from his hiding place in the fake weed, where he was just an orange blob amongst the green-feathered plastic, his golden fins beating rhythmically in the still water.

"There are lights and stuff outside the window," said James, cricking his neck to look up at the ceiling. "And there's something on the roof!" Breaking into a prickly sweat, he grabbed the heavy, rubber torch that lay under his bed.

When Mendel did eventually speak, his words struck terror in James's heart. "Oh dear, it looks like Sleven has decided to pay us a visit after all."

This was the last thing James wanted to hear.

Mendel sounded surprisingly calm in the circumstances. "James, you must go outside now. I need you to get as close as you can to this monster."

"What!" James wheezed his reply, gobsmacked at the idea.

Mendel continued to give his terrifying instructions as though he was merely reading out some vaguely amusing story, the kind slotted into the end of a nasty news bulletin in a useless attempt to cheer you up. "Now get yourself outside and we'll find out whether my mind-merge has worked. If it has taken, I should be able to do my magic through you."

James was annoyed by Mendel's blasé tone. "And if it hasn't?" he demanded.

A large, blue flash shook the room, removing the opportunity for Mendel to answer.

A slate fell past the leaded windowpane.

"James, you need to trust me. Go outside!" Mendel's voice seemed to lead him – to force him – onwards.

Outside, James steadied himself on the coalbunker and shone his rubber torch up into the weird, multicoloured mist engulfing his house.

"Time-trance," said James in a fishy, bubbly voice. And again, only louder, "Time-trance!"

His face flushed as he tried to mouth the fishy words. They actually sounded more like "Twiwimwmwetwrawnwcwe...", as if he were speaking while pinging his lips up and down with his fore-finger.

The knock-knock-knocking sensation had returned, making James feel as if he had cold lumps of ice bumping against each other inside his head.

But the spell – as James guessed it was – changed nothing.

The swirling lights raced even faster over James's roof until the colours rushed together to form a blinding flash of pure white. Red and yellow dots spun round at the back of James's eyes, but he could still see well enough to spot a strange, misshapen creature coming toward him. "Sleven," he whispered to himself.

Sleven had a toad-like head that seemed far too heavy for his skinny neck. But, unlike any toad, his mouth contained row upon row of needle-sharp teeth. Yellow, steaming slime dripped from them.

Sleven was neither a man nor any kind of creature James had ever seen before.

Craning his neck to look up at Sleven's evil, slit-like eyes, the torch wavered in his hand, causing a strobe effect that made Sleven look even more horrid.

Spying James, Sleven jerked his oversized head back in a series of grotesque twitches that caused him to temporarily lose his footing.

James gulped when he saw the size of Sleven's feet. Extremely elongated, each one had three skinny toes that wiggled like spider's legs as the creature struggled to keep his balance on the slates. Sleven hissed with annoyance and gripped onto the ridging of the roof.

Watching Sleven as he tried to steady himself, James

saw that he had no ears, only two gaping holes that ran from where his ears should have been, down towards his hideously toothed jaw. The drool that dripped from the side of his mouth splashed onto the ice-cold slates, causing small clouds of steam to rise up through sparks that danced round his long, twisted legs.

Slowly, Sleven tilted his big head and focused in on James. He hissed a spit-laden jumble of words that sounded like, "Wheresss iss Mendelssss?"

James whimpered as the monster continued to blink in his direction. He didn't know what to say.

The torch slipped from James's fingers and clunked onto the ground. But then, instead of fear, he felt an overwhelming anger begin to burn inside him: a warm glow that started in his chest and quickly moved down his arms to his fingertips. He looked the beast in the eye, showing courage he didn't know he possessed, and said, "What have you done with my dad?"

Only briefly distracted by James's question, Sleven sucked in a huge strand of glistening drool that wobbled from the side of his mouth, then leapt down from the roof. He bounced onto the ground and swung a long skinny arm at James's throat. Three razor-sharp claws sliced through the bitter night air, missing him by inches.

James opened his mouth to scream but the word "time-trance", followed rapidly by "snuff-light", burst from his lips instead.

Mid-pounce, Sleven froze, split into a million pieces, and collapsed back in on himself with a blinding blue flash.

James took a sharp breath and fumbled for his torch. He traced the beam over the garden and then back over the roof but there was no sign of Sleven. All that remained was an eggy, sulphurous, farty stink that made James cough and gag.

"What *was* that thing?" James wheezed before covering his mouth.

Oddly, Mendel's voice, when it came into James's head, was tinged with sadness. "That poor wretch belonged to a race that once possessed the most ancient of magic powers, but..." he paused, "...I fear Sleven was the last of his kind. The Swamp Troll – *Sygentius Trolificus* to be precise – is now extinct."

"Well, good riddance," James snorted. He immediately sensed Mendel's disapproval, but was too troubled by the stench to really care. "What is that *smell*?"

"Smell...? What smell?" said Mendel.

James began to make his way back towards the front door. "So, you can see what I can see, but you can't smell what I can smell?"

"It would seem that way, wouldn't it?" said Mendel.

"Lucky you!" said James, pinching his nose. He could hear Mendel splashing about and hoped the fish wasn't spilling bathwater over his newly polished pine floor. Sleven was scary, but his mum was a nightmare.

"James," said Mendel, "we have a problem with your friend."

"What, Craig?" exclaimed James, stopping at the front door to peer down Willow Terrace.

"He has the crystal," announced Mendel.

"How do you know that?" asked James, waving traces of coloured mist away from his face.

"Trust me, he has the crystal, and we need to use it before anything else comes through the gateway," said Mendel.

James wondered what gateway Mendel was talking about. Were more magical creatures like Sleven going to come after them? What had Mendel done to deserve this?

Teeth chattering in the cold Drumfintley dawn, James looked up at his mum's bedroom window and whispered to himself, "She'll go crazy if she finds me out here."

Mendel's voice sounded tired. "Your mother is completely unaware that you're outside and—"

"James!" an irate voice interrupted. "What are you doing outside in your pyjamas? With no shoes on? Do you know what time it is?" His mum peered down at him from her bedroom window.

"I was getting the milk, Mum." James knew it was a pathetic lie, but was quietly impressed with himself for saying something at least half believable.

"At four in the morning?"

James gulped.

"The milk's not even here yet! Get inside right this minute, you idiot! You're grounded tomorrow as well!"

She yelled so loud that several lights flicked on in the terrace. A sleeping cat, which had been lying on Mr Fyffe's wall, fell off into a steel bin with a *Bang! Meow! Sssssssss...*

James's heart felt like an anvil. There was no way his mum would calm down now. She'd be like this for at least the next two days.

How does she get the energy to be so angry for so long? he wondered.

Cathy Peck pushed her head further out of her window and continued her rant, "Get to your bed! Wash your feet first! You're just like your dad...a complete numpty!"

As the word 'numpty' echoed off the red brick walls of the houses on the opposite side of the street, a few *more* lights flicked on.

Whenever his mum yelled at him, there were always four or five commands, questions and statements mixed up in one venomous screech. Never knowing what to do first, he inevitably took too long to pick out the most important piece of information and ended up getting yelled at even more.

"Don't just stand there, gawping! Get inside! And

what's..." She pinched her nose. "What's that smell?" She slammed her window shut.

Across the street, Ephie Blake's net curtains twitched.

Before James reached the top of the stairs, he heard his mum slam her bedroom door shut. The timber-frame house was still shaking when Mendel spoke again in James's head. "Your mother is feeling down."

"Down?" whispered James. "That's the understatement of the century. We definitely have to find a way of saving your skin, or scales, or whatever it is we're doing, without disturbing my mum again. Can't you put a Nice Person spell on her? Or a Mute spell?"

"I can't do that, James," said Mendel, "Your mother has every right to be angry. I mean, you shouldn't be out at this time of night anyway, should you?"

"But *you're* the one who wanted me to go out there in the first place," James spluttered. For the second time in twenty-four hours, he felt like tipping the annoying little fish right down the toilet.

Mendel's tone was conciliatory. "Yes, I suppose. But in your mother's eyes..."

"I'm just a pest," said James, breaking into an asthmatic cough.

"Stop coughing!" his mum yelled from under her covers, making him try to hold his breath.

"She doesn't know what's happening," said Mendel. "And I get the impression that she is a little depressed."

"Depressed?" hissed James. He looked down at his mud-encrusted feet. "What about me? I miss my dad more than she does."

Suddenly weary, James slumped down on his bed and gazed up at the blue and white neckerchiefs that crisscrossed his bedroom wall.

"Mendel, if I help you to get back home, find that talisman thing, do you promise to help me find my dad?"

he asked, yawning loudly, his eyelids like a pair of lead aprons.

Mendel's voice became fuzzy as sleep swept over James. "I will try. I just hope that your friend Craig has been very careful with the crystal. Otherwise we are both dead already."

James, however, had drifted off in a series of sniffs and snores.

7

Cupboards and Smells

James opened one eye and stared at the digital clock. It was one minute past eight. As slowly as he could, he turned his head, opened the other eye, then looked across his bedroom floor. Like an ugly wart, the old, bashed tin bath was still there, and all the horrors of the night before flooded back into his mind.

The coughing began quietly, but rapidly grew into the usual early morning crescendo that often resulted in James being physically sick.

The bedroom wall soon reverberated with the sound of his mum's knocking. "Shut up! I'm trying to sleep!" She'd never been the Florence Nightingale type.

James sat bolt upright as the sensation of drowning increased. Then, as he shook his head in an effort to clear his airways, a bubbly noise – "Wwweezwwungwww" – spluttered from his lips.

He gasped, then drew in a lungful of wonderfully fresh air. As quickly as it had begun, his coughing fit stopped. The drowning sensation evaporated. He could actually straighten his back. The sweat and panic drifted away too. He felt as though he could run all the way to the Jesus Rocks and back without once fumbling for his inhaler.

He whisked his legs out from under his duvet and spun round to face the rusty tin bath. "Mendel?" He waited for the wizard's voice.

"Good morning, James."

"You… you made my asthma go away. My cough's gone."

The googly-eyed goldfish came into view. "Feeling

better?"

James stood up and stretched his arms above his head. "I feel fantastic! I can breathe without wheezing. Listen!" James stooped over the bath and took a large breath of cold, morning air. "Nothing. No rattle or whine. How—"

"—did I do it?" Mendel finished.

James screwed up his face in annoyance, but the wizard-goldfish had made his asthma go away and that really counted for something.

Mendel swam into view. "What you call asthma is simply an irritation of the bronchiole mucus membrane that results in a reduction in the diameter of the airways, which results in the build-up of discharge, which results in a sensation of—"

This time James interrupted Mendel. "—drowning."

Mendel circled his plastic castle. "Quite!"

James hadn't really understood Mendel's explanation. Neither was he sure that the fish wizard had actually answered his question, but no matter what magic Mendel had performed, or would ever perform, to James nothing would surpass this.

There was a click, click, clicking sound from the tin bath. James peered down to see Mendel mouthing bits of grit and stone from the bottom.

"Yuck!" he exclaimed. "What are you doing?"

"It's a fish thing," said Mendel. "It helps me think." Mendel's voice sounded irritated and restless now. "Your friend definitely has the crystal. I can sense it."

"You already said that last night. You were also going to say something about my dad, but you never finished," said James pointedly.

Mendel swam close to the surface, flipping his tail with a splash before zooming to the bottom of the bath again. "The crystal, if used properly, is a kind of key. It can make the stone circle on Bruce Moor function as a gateway."

"Are you saying…that my dad has gone to another place? To your world?"

"It's a possibility. Either by accident or…"

"Or what?" James's eyes widened.

"Or he's been taken there." Mendel weaved between the fake weeds.

"On purpose? Why would anyone take my dad?" James half expected to start wheezing any second and, through habit, picked up his inhaler, just in case.

"I'll explain everything once you bring me the crystal, James. There's no time to waste. So for now, you'll just have to do as I say. Before you go, however, please remember these three things…" Mendel's bulging orange eye appeared above the surface of the water. "Do *not* unwrap the crystal. Do *not* touch the crystal with your bare hands and, most importantly, do *not* expose the crystal to sunlight." Mendel flicked his orange tail three times, as if to emphasise each point, before slipping back beneath the surface.

James felt a building sense of foreboding. "You didn't say any of this yesterday."

Mendel didn't reply.

If Craig had the crystal, James would bet all the tea in China that his friend had broken all three rules already. He had to do something.

* * *

Unfortunately, the bits and pieces that made up his real life could not be ignored. It was all very well for Mendel to tell him to go and get the crystal, but James had chores, homework and especially his mum to think about. It was a Sunday and he had church, the weekly breakfast trip to his crazy Aunt Bella's and, oh yes, he was 'grrrounded'.

Perhaps if he told his mum what was going on she might let him go. How might he put it…? *Mum, a magic goldfish has just cured my asthma and says monsters have abducted Dad. So I'm off to Craig's to fetch a magic crystal. Okay?*

Yeah, right!

No, he would just have to risk going to Craig's house without permission. *How am I going to get to his house without being seen?*

"There's no choice, James," Mendel piped up again.

James let out a long sigh. "Can't I even think without you jumping into my head?"

He could still hear the goldfish rearranging the grit in the bath.

It was still only ten past eight in the morning and his mum would be dozing for at least another twenty minutes. He might be able to pull it off if he left right away. He didn't really have a choice. If he was going to help his dad, he had to try.

After slipping on a pair of football shorts and a new white shirt, James opened his bedroom window and stretched down the four feet or so until his feet brushed the coal bunker below. It was still damp, and he slipped on the mossy lid that sloped towards the lawn. With a small yelp, he bashed off the bunker and squelched onto the soaking wet grass.

Standing up slowly, James looked down at his sodden shorts. It looked – and felt – like he'd wet himself.

As the cold morning air hit his chest, he braced himself for the inevitable coughing fit, but when nothing happened he smiled and punched the air triumphantly. *Has my asthma really gone for good?*

Uncomfortably wet, yet still exhilarated, James waddled towards the back fence as fast as he could. He ducked through a well-worn gap and edged behind Mr Fyffe's car.

Hauling up his cold, wet shorts, he scanned the street for signs of life. There was nothing except a few nervous cats, and a seagull picking at an abandoned poke of chips. James eased out from behind the car and then belted past Ephie Blake's house.

* * *

Craig's house was semi-detached, roughcast and rundown. Normally, the only way up to his best friend's bedroom – apart from the stairs – was to scramble up a dodgy plastic drainpipe at the back of the house, but since James was soaking and would probably slip and hurt himself, he instead picked up a handful of tiny stones and lobbed them at Craig's window. A few hit the glass, but the rest landed back in James's hair. One or two even slid down his neck and found their way into his soggy shorts.

"Craig!" he whispered as loudly as he dared. "Crai— Arrghhh." This time his forced whisper turned into a yowl as a big, yellow, furry thing with bad breath pounced on him. Another monster must have made its way through the moor's stone circle...

"Bero!" he yelled. "Gerrofff!"

Bero had him pinned to the ground in a Golden Retriever death grip. James couldn't move and the old dog was drooling long strands of slobber onto his nose. He thought back to Sleven and shivered.

"Get off me, you big brute," James panted.

"Bero!" Craig's voice called out from above. "In! Now!" Craig peered down and shook his head. "Y' numpty! Look at the state of you! What's happened? Why so early?" Craig homed in on James's wet shorts. "You haven't...have you?"

James frowned. "No, I bloomin' have not. Just let me in," he snapped.

Craig grinned, ducked inside and came down to meet him.

Amazingly, Craig's mum, Jean, had slept through the

whole episode. So, accompanied by Bero, they slipped into Craig's poster-papered room, shutting the door behind them as quietly as they could. James turned to sit on the bed but Craig stopped him. "Uh-uh." Craig waved a finger at James and pointed to his dripping shorts. "I don't want any stinky wee on my bed."

James pointed his own finger of warning. "I told you..."

"Whatever," sighed Craig.

James remained standing. "Did you get the blue crystal?" He took note of the time on Craig's digital clock. It read 08:21.

"You mean that weird prism thing?"

James nodded, although he'd never actually seen the crystal himself.

"Yeah, of course I did. It's in the cupboard." Craig opened a flimsy, white door.

Inside, James saw a bundle of dirty blue cloth.

"How do you know it looks like a prism?" he asked, growing worried. Then, as Craig bent down to pick it up, he shouted, "Stop!"

But the cloth had already fallen to the floor.

"Cool your jets!" hissed Craig. "You'll wake Mum."

"For goodness' sake, cover it up!" James squeaked, his anxiety rising.

"*You* cover it up, ye ungrateful..." Craig tossed the crystal towards James.

James automatically sidestepped the flying crystal, then stared in horror as it bounced onto the bed. Hesitating for a moment, he snatched it up and frantically looked about the bedroom.

Without a care in the world, Craig toyed with Bero's floppy brown ear as James yanked a plastic supermarket bag from under the bed and forced the crystal inside.

"Okay," he began shakily, "it's not just for some Geography project."

"No kidding," said Craig.

James flushed. "I'll tell you more soon, but I need to get back home before my mum wakes up."

Craig picked up the dirty blue cloth and threw it back into his cupboard. "Tell me now."

"I can't," said James.

Craig shook his head. "You know, it's hardly worth being pals with you. Your nut of a mum's got you permanently grounded."

James saw Bero's ears flatten just before he heard Errol, the paperboy, trying to stuff the Sunday supplement through the letterbox downstairs.

Bero exploded into a series of barks and growls.

"I'll explain later, Craig. I promise," James said over the din.

Without looking back, James edged down the stairs and flattened himself against the wall. He held onto Bero's collar until Errol had gone, then slipped outside.

"You'd better tell me!" Craig shouted after him.

"I promise!" said James, his voice trailing off as he shot up Craig's garden path.

Turning round the corner of Craig's house, James failed to avoid the little present left earlier by Bero. He slipped on the mess, but managed to regain his step and keep running.

"Thanks, Bero," he muttered as he ran up the path toward Willow Terrace. To his dismay, he was beginning to wheeze again and the sharp stones in his wet boxers were jagging his bum.

He glanced back at the clock on St Donan's church tower.

Three minutes to go.

As he bolted up his garden path and dashed into the garage, he prayed that his mum was still sleeping. "Where is it?" he mumbled as he fumbled about on a shelf above his head. An assortment of washers and nails showered him but, eventually, he found the spare backdoor key. It felt cold in his hand.

One minute!

He slid into the kitchen, kicked off his poo-encrusted trainers, opened the washing machine, stripped off his filthy shirt, and was just about to chuck his shorts into the wash drum when the kitchen door swung open behind him.

"James!" His mum had the look of a beast about to pounce. "What are you doing standing in the kitchen with no clothes on?" she hissed.

James opened his mouth but nothing came out.

8

Denthan

The blue crystal lay next to Mendel's tin bath. Partly concealed by an old pair of swimming trunks and still wrapped in the supermarket carrier bag, James had made sure that the large gem remained well protected from the sunlight filtering through his bedroom window.

Mendel congratulated him. "You did well to bring the crystal here so soon."

"Yes, well now I'm grounded for two days instead of one, and Craig is totally confused. I have to tell him *some*thing." Exhausted, James pulled on his socks and forced his heels into his new black shoes.

Bang, Bang, Click.

He thumped the floor until the stiff leather finally gave way and his foot slipped into position. He hated messing about with laces.

"Mendel, I think my asthma is coming back," he said.

"Ah well, you see, that spell was only a quick fix. I would need my own laboratory and a good deal of time to give you permanent freedom from your curse." There was a hint of frustration in Mendel's voice. "And time is a luxury we don't have."

James sprinkled some fish food on the water and watched the wizard-goldfish make his way to the surface. His plump, fishy lips mouthed "mpah, mpah, mpah" as he bit and nibbled at the blue and red flakes. Between mouthfuls Mendel asked, "Where...is the...blue cloth... that protected the crystal?"

James kicked the crystal further under the rim of the

bath and wondered how to answer the wizard without making him angry. "It was all a bit rushed in Craig's house so I think it may have been left behind."

Mendel stopped eating. "So you exposed the crystal to the light?"

James knew the wizard could read his thoughts, so there was no point in lying. "We might have done," he answered tentatively.

Disgruntled, Mendel said, "Didn't you remember the three things that I told you? You can't begin to understand what we're dealing with here." It was the first time Mendel had raised his voice in such a way.

"It wasn't a case of *remembering* anything," said James, "since you didn't tell me about those three rules until it was too late! And no, I have no idea what we're dealing with here, because you won't *tell* me. You haven't explained anything about the stranger, or my dad!"

Mendel replied with a resigned sigh. "Place the crystal, inadequate wrappings and all, into the bath."

As James lowered the heavy crystal into the water, Mendel tried to explain.

"I was sent here from a place called Denthan."

"Where's that?" James could not recall seeing it on a map.

"It's my home. My world."

"Your..." James was still coming to grips with a talking fish, never mind another world. "Wait, isn't Denthan the place I heard the stranger talking about?"

"Most probably."

"So, who's he?"

"I'll come to him soon enough." Mendel swam towards the crystal. "The dice have been cast, James, which unfortunately means your world and mine are now in terrible danger." Circling, Mendel looked up at James with his big, googly eyes. "When pointed in the right direction, and on saying the correct spell, this crystal will take us back to Denthan."

"*Us*? You mean I need to come *with* you?" James stared down into the water.

Mendel stopped swimming. His gills opened and closed a few times before he said, "I can't do any magic without you, James, and I need you to identify the talisman. Without it I cannot perform what I *must* perform. You see, now that we've made the connection, our fates are inextricably intertwined."

James was horror-struck. "I'm not sure what you mean. Are you saying...whatever happens to you happens to me?"

"In a way, yes."

James bit his lip. "And my dad...how does he fit into all this?"

"My suspicion is that your father was simply in the wrong place at the wrong time. He is gone, but your heart tells me that he is still alive."

"How can it do that?" James knelt down beside the tin bath.

Mendel took a moment to consider this before saying, tentatively, "Well, now that I'm connected to you, I am able to tell that you are still connected to him, just as you are to your mother. I suspect your father may have been drawn through to my world."

Wheezing loudly, James reached for his inhaler.

Mendel waited for James to take his medicine before continuing. "If you help me now, there's a chance we may find your father. You see, I was sent here, in this form, as a kind of punishment...punishment for something that I discovered."

"Who sent you? Sleven and the stranger?"

"In a way," said Mendel. "But I need to tell you a story to explain it properly."

"Well, tell it then."

James sat himself next to the tin bath and waited in anticipation. Mendel swam away from the crystal and circled the plastic castle.

"Where I come from," began Mendel, "we were lucky enough to have a kind and noble King called Athelstone. He was loved and revered by his people and all was well until, one day, he went hunting in a great forest called Eldane. While chasing a black stag, the King became separated from his entourage, and although his horse returned, he did not. We searched for weeks but eventually resigned ourselves to the probability that he'd been killed. Finding no trace of either the King or his clothing we presumed that he'd been caught unawares by some beast of the forest.

"Then, two years after his disappearance, and quite unexpectedly, King Athelstone appeared at our city gates. Still dressed in the same hunting clothes, he looked to be totally unharmed."

"Where had he been?" asked James, eager to hear how this story might connect to his dad's disappearance.

"He said that he'd lost his memory," Mendel replied, "but that was not the truth." He looked up at James. "Everyone was so overjoyed at his return that they overlooked a major possibility."

"What was that?" asked James.

"That he wasn't the same person. The real Athelstone, the one I knew and had saved years before from a Wrafnar, was marked by his confrontation with the beast."

"A Wrafnar?" James enquired.

"An immortal assassin that can never be stopped once he is on someone's trail."

"Ah," sighed James, none the wiser.

"I banished the creature to another place just in time, but the King had been wounded. I alone knew about the

King's scar. A deep slash he suffered to his lower arm. From time to time it would weep black blood, as you cannot completely heal a wound from a Wrafnar, but the King concealed it well. He didn't want the rest of the counsellors to know about his affliction."

"So," said James, his mind racing, "the new King didn't have this wound."

"The mark was there but he often had it in full view, and it never wept or flared up. I knew then that this Athelstone was, and still is, an impostor; a Hedra wizard called Dendralon. He alone can perform the dark Hedra magic that allows a wizard to wear and live within the skin of the dead; our dead King's skin. He is intent on leading our people to their doom."

"But you must have tried to tell people – to confront him?" said James.

Mendel splashed his golden tail. "I tried, and that is why I am in this mess."

"Is he the one...?" began James.

"That you call 'the stranger'?" said Mendel, splashing to the surface. "Yes. He is the one who sent me here, James. Everything that has happened to you, and possibly your father, is linked to him. We have to get back to Denthan to stop him before it's too late."

"So he took my dad? Why?" pressed James.

Before Mendel could answer, an irate voice called up from the bottom of the stairs. "James! It's time for church. Now! And don't force your feet into your new shoes!"

James glanced guiltily at his battered-looking shoes. He often wondered if his mum really *was* a witch. She always seemed to know what he was doing.

"Okay," he called down to her. Then, waving a hand over the bath, he said to Mendel, "I have to go out for a while."

"But you can't!" Mendel protested. "I'm not sure it's safe."

"I haven't got any choice," James complained. "I won't be safe from Mum if I don't go right now."

Mendel swished his tail in annoyance. "Be careful. The reason you felt strange when you wandered into the stone circle yesterday was because Dendralon will have sent others through the gateway to do his dirty work. He needs to finish me off before I find a way to return and expose him.

"It was only because of my position, my high standing in Denthan, that he couldn't kill me there. He would have lost the trust of the High Council. So he had to settle for a morphic banishment."

"A morphic what?" James shook his head in frustration.

"James! Who are you talking to?" his mum demanded from downstairs.

"No one, Mum," he shouted back.

Mendel continued talking to him as he made his way down the stairs. "A morphic banishment is when you're sent through a gateway in the form of an innocuous creature to live out a pitiful life on some other world. Dendralon will know by now that you are helping me, James, so be careful. Be very careful."

"I need to go," James answered, a mingling of fear and frustration building in his chest.

Interpreting his words as a question, his mum clipped him round the ear. "Of course you need to go! We always go to church."

* * *

Less than halfway up the garden path James began to feel a twinge in his stomach. He screwed up his face and paused at the gate. His hand clasped a rusting rail as he bent double in pain.

"Be quick!" snapped his mum, marching out onto the

road. Seeing him grip the gate, however, she sighed and turned on her heels. She tilted her head and gave him a curious look. "Don't start," she warned. "Father Michael is coming to give us a lift. You better not show me up."

The pain was getting worse and James glanced back up at his bedroom window. Was this anything to do with Mendel? The wizard had warned him not to go.

A bottle-green car that looked like an antique spluttered to a stop outside their house. "What's wrong with our own car?" whimpered James.

"What's wrong with *you*?" his mum hissed back.

James didn't know. It felt as if there was a swarm of bees in his stomach. Eyes watering, he glanced down the street, over the rooftops.

"All set?" enquired Father Michael, a wispy-haired, balding man with a nervous smile. He wore a jacket with patches on the elbows and a white 'dog collar' that made his chin jut out at an awkward angle.

"Of course," said Cathy, urging James on with a particularly nasty frown.

It was then that James heard a loud crack, distant but pronounced. His jaw dropped open as he fixed his gaze on St Donan's spire. There was something in the sky above the church. His eyes were telling him that the gargoyle on the west wall of the church tower had broken away from the building and was flapping high above Drumfintley.

Through his pain he bit his lip and pointed past Father Michael towards the creature.

His mum, however, was too busy trying to prize his fingers from the rusty garden fence and Father Michael was inspecting his mum's car.

"You say it's making a funny noise," he said, kneeling and peering under the exhaust pipe.

"Yes," hissed his mum, still hauling at James.

James yelped and made to run back into the house but

his mum caught his sleeve.

The gargoyle, flapping slowly but methodically in their direction, let out a terrible cry. It had the face of a deranged dog and an array of spikes covered its leathery skin. Like a jaggy Doberman with bats' wings, it eventually slowed and hovered over their garden.

"Mum!" screamed James, but neither his mum nor Father Michael seemed aware of the danger.

The gargoyle was only a few feet above their heads.

"What's gotten into you?" asked his mum.

Father Michael gave James a quizzical stare. "What's wrong with him, Cathy?"

"Just help me loosen his grip!" she barked.

Between them, they jerked James away from the fence and out onto the street.

The gargoyle roared above him and stretched down with talons the size of meat hooks.

James screamed and pulled away.

Father Michael smiled sympathetically and helped his mum pull James back towards the cars. "It's only church, son," he joked. "My sermons aren't *that* bad."

The gargoyle twisted round on its leathery wings and snapped down with its black teeth. It still looked like a lump of heavy sandstone, but it moved like a living animal.

James yanked free of his mum, sweat running into his eyes. He tried to wriggle away from Father Michael, but the young vicar held him tight. In panic, James spun and kicked hard.

Father Michael let go immediately, screamed, and fell to his knees, clutching his groin.

Cathy Peck screamed too, mortified with embarrassment. "What are you trying to do to me?" she yelped.

The air whooshed past James's face as the creature's wings beat above him. The gargoyle dropped down towards him, its stench preceding it. James braced himself as the world around him spun. His chest was tight, he couldn't breathe, his head pounded.

An all-enveloping curtain of darkness began to smother him. He closed his eyes as pain racked his body. He tried to speak – "It's too heavy... Mendel... Mum..." he muttered, before drawing a final sharp breath and blurting "Wwwstonewwwrightwww!"

9

The Journey Begins

Standing outside the Harrison's house, Cathy Peck could hear Joe and Helen, Craig's younger brother and sister, arguing over which cartoon channel to watch. She pressed the doorbell and listened, irritably, as it whirred, clattered and eventually made a small ding.

She saw Craig's mother, Jean, through the frosted glass and felt a little surge of adrenaline as the door swung open.

"Hello, Cathy!" Jean greeted her with a nervous smile spreading across her freckled face.

Cathy didn't know Jean particularly well, but she knew that David was bound to have met her at one of his precious Scout meetings.

"If it's about David..." Jean blurted.

"I'm actually here about James," said Cathy.

"Oh," began Jean.

Cathy straightened. "You haven't noticed him acting strangely, have you?"

Jean Harrison looked like a startled hare. Cathy knew why, of course.

"I expect he...eh...has been acting a bit strange...what with...you know..."

With Jean's wide, sympathetic eyes staring at her, Cathy was finding it hard to say what she really wanted to say.

Seeing Cathy struggle, Jean's expression mellowed further. "You'd better come in."

Cathy followed her into the living room and sat down.

"Coffee?" Without waiting for an answer, Jean dashed

into the kitchen and returned in seconds with a big tray. She poured some coffee into a chipped mug, then eased herself into a red, leather chair, all ears.

Munching on a chocolate teacake, Cathy reeled off the incident outside her house, explaining how James had passed out after felling Father Michael.

"Why on earth did he do that?" asked Jean, moving over to the drinks cabinet.

Cathy ignored the question. "When Father Michael recovered enough to go to the church, he had to walk. His car was covered in red sand and it wouldn't start. Goodness knows where that came from." She told Jean how she'd phoned Doctor Miller and how he'd said that James was probably suffering from something called Delayed Stress Syndrome. "I even caught him wandering around in the front garden last night at four in the morning."

"Oh, dear," whispered Jean.

"I just wondered if Craig had noticed anything out of the ordinary."

Jean popped her head into the hall. "Craig! Darling!"

Craig trundled into the front room and, when questioned, explained that James was fine 'under the circumstances', perhaps a bit hyper, but basically normal enough. "Can I go out for a bit?" he asked his mum. "I'll take Bero."

Jean, already fussing round Cathy, flicked him away with a wiggle of her painted nails.

* * *

In number forty-five Willow Terrace, James heard someone banging up the stairs.

"James, are you up there? Your mum's in our house asking questions about you."

"Come up," he groaned. His head was still fragile.

Craig barged into his bedroom and instantly stared at the tin bath.

Bero gave a doggy sigh and plumped down, disinterested, in the corner of the room.

Craig knelt beside the bath. "Cool." He stuck his finger in the water.

"Don't touch it!" James cried, sensing he was going to need Mendel's help with this. He would never be able to explain everything. "Look, it's my dad. He might be in danger."

Craig pulled his hand out of the bath and flicked some of the water onto James's face. "Wake up and smell the roses, James! Your dad's run off because your mum's a fruit and nut case. And you, my Scottish numpty, are losing it big time."

James felt a flash of frustration. He tensed as his head began to pound, and then... "Swnwwakewwwritheww!"

Craig frowned. "Why are you trying to sound like you're underwater? What the...?"

Suddenly, Craig's hands began to twitch and his forearms started to shake.

James saw his friend wince as his skin turned bright yellow, then yelp as his arms transformed into two twisting, spitting snakes.

Black tongues flicked in and out of the snakes' yellow-scaled mouths and their fangs dripped pus-coloured venom as they spat and snapped round Craig's horror-stricken face.

"James!" screeched Craig. "Stop them!"

"Eh..." James replied nervously, the wizard's voice echoing in his head. "Mendel says they can't harm you."

"Who? Just stop them!" Craig looked totally manic.

Then, just as James thought Craig was about to pass out, he felt the knocking sensation build inside his head again. "Swwnuffww Swnwwakeww."

The yellow scales turned pink, the snakeheads changed back into fingers, and the writhing, reptilian bodies jerked back into the shape of two quite normal arms.

Tiny beads of sweat rolled down Craig's forehead and onto his cheeks as he stood transfixed, staring in stunned silence at James. "What h... h... h... happened?" He glanced down at his arms before gingerly peering over the side of the tin bath.

James followed his gaze and saw Mendel swimming in lazy circles, looking entirely innocent. With little effort, his shimmering orange tail slowly propelled him between the plastic castle and a clump of fake weed.

"I must have caught whatever you have. Or... or... it's some kind of illusion, right?" Craig gave up and dropped to his knees.

"I need to tell you something really weird." James knelt beside his friend and stared down at the pulsating goldfish. "This is Mendel. He can do magic and he talks to me. That is, I hear him in my head and, well, that's pretty much it."

Mendel chose that moment to speak up. "I believe you can both hear me now."

Craig and James looked at each other.

"Craig," Mendel continued without waiting for confirmation, "everything James has said so far is true."

Craig glanced round the room, searching for the source of the voice.

Mendel spoke again. "I have to ask you a question, Craig."

"Fire away," said Craig in a shaky voice.

"When you dug up the crystal, did you expose it to the sunlight?"

"No."

"Did you touch it with your bare hands?" pressed Mendel.

James saw Mendel's fins tense.

"No," Craig said again.

James turned to his friend. "This could be important, Craig."

"Well, you never said anything about not touching it or exposing it to the light, did you?" Craig accused sulkily.

"I know, but think. Yes or no?" James knew the look on his friend's face. He'd seen it too many times. James held his gaze, patiently waiting for Craig to crack. He always did.

"Fine! Yes, yes, yes. So what?"

Mendel's voice, when he spoke again, was sombre. "Look carefully at the surface of the water and you will see why this is so important."

James massaged his temples as the knock, knock, knocking sensation began again. "Wwwvisionww-poolwww," spilled like a sigh from his lips.

In response to his command, the surface of the bath water turned blood red, flashed blue, then transformed into a smooth mirror. For several moments, silver streaks of mist swirled over the surface until a small flash of lightning lit up the room.

They were soon looking down at a crystal-clear picture. It showed a blond, messy-haired little boy in brown shorts and a blue jumper that was too big for him. Beside him, a tall, solid, blond girl in jeans and pink hoodie was sticking her tongue out.

"It's my brother and sister, Wee Joe and Helen!" Craig exclaimed. "And they're mucking about with the TV in my room! Just wait until I get my hands on those little brats."

In the vision pool, Helen snatched the remote from Wee Joe's grasping hands.

"Mum!" Wee Joe bellowed like a wounded bull. "Mum! Helen has—"

"Shhhh, Joe! Look at me!" Helen pleaded. "Look at this!"

Having snatched the remote, it appeared to dawn on her that there might be consequences. She immediately stood on her head in an effort to transform Wee Joe's screams of annoyance into screams of laughter. "Look! I'm an upside-down, farty pig," she said, in a piggy voice. "Ssnnyorrrt! Nkuuk!"

There was a zapping sound and the picture in the vision pool suddenly shifted to Craig's downstairs living room. There, Craig's mum, seemingly embarrassed by the interruption upstairs, stared at the spot on the ceiling where the racket was coming from, and yelled in a posh nanny tone, "Helen, Darling. What are you doing?" Flushing pink, Jean smiled at Cathy and mouthed "sorry" several times.

By this time, back in the upstairs bedroom, Joe was screaming with laughter, the remote returned to his grubby little fingers along with two Blackjack sweets.

Another zap and the view switched back to his mum and Cathy Peck in the living room.

"I've got enough on my plate with the Police and everyone else nattering about me, without James...

Oh, Constable Watt's alright," Craig's mum said, "just a bit on the keen side. I'm sure he doesn't really think that you had anything to do with David's disappearance, not directly."

Cathy Peck let her teaspoon clatter onto the saucer. "What do you mean, 'not directly'?"

Jean eased back. "Well, you know what men are like. They need their space and..."

"Space?" Cathy's voice became threatening. "Well, as far as I'm concerned, the sooner James and I move on the better!"

Jean flushed. "I'm sure there's a—"

"—perfectly reasonable explanation?" finished Cathy. "For his sake, he'd better be dead. Because if he's just up and left, I'll kill him! Slowly..." she added, twisting the wrapper of her second chocolate teacake until it snapped in two.

* * *

"This is better than any TV show...ever," breathed Craig.

James couldn't take any more. "That's enough, Mendel!"

The fish-wizard cleared his throat. "As you wish, James."

There was a small flash on the surface, then a luminous digital clock appeared at the bottom of the picture and began whirring through the seconds.

"Just say when!" Mendel pronounced.

"Eh? When!" Craig blurted out.

The picture froze. "Now, most importantly: how long?"

James gulped. "What are you talking about?"

"How long do you want each loop to last?" said Mendel.

"What loop?" asked James.

"The time loop," said Mendel impatiently. "Thirty minutes is the maximum. I'll fix it at that." The moment Cathy Peck bit into her third chocolate teacake the picture froze. The display read 19:15:01, exactly.

"Now that you've marked the beginning of the loop," Mendel explained, "the seconds will tick by until 19:45:01, at which point time will return to 19:15:01 and begin again. Simple, right?"

"Eh, nope." James shrugged. There seemed to be nothing simple about it.

Mendel rolled his large, fishy eyes. "We need to get to the Jesus Rocks. They're the gateway I talked of, the one that leads to my world. If we don't get there soon, both our worlds are doomed, especially now that Craig has, rather stupidly, revealed his inner thoughts to our enemy."

James fixed his best friend an accusing stare.

"By setting this time loop," Mendel continued, "we have given ourselves the perfect alibi. No one will know we're gone." The wizard looked up from the bath. "I'm just trying to make things a little easier with your parents. I'll look after you. I promise."

James began to work it out. It was Sunday, the twenty-second of June, and apparently, until Mendel broke the spell, the half-hour loop would repeat itself until they'd all made their way, undisturbed, to the ancient standing stones on Bruce Moor.

"What about transport?" asked Craig, pointing at Mendel. "How do we get a goldfish up to the Jesus Rocks?"

James looked round his room then reached under his bed until he found what he was looking for. "We could fill this see-through water wing with some of the bath water and put him inside. Then all we have to do is slide him over my arm," he suggested, slowly slipping into a 'maybe that does sound kinda daft' voice.

"I don't think so," Mendel replied.

Craig too looked puzzled by the suggestion. "How would we get him inside the bloomin' thing in the first place?"

"Well, I don't know!" said James defensively. "I guess that's why he was sent here as a fish. Not too easy to get around."

"Not easy at all," Mendel agreed. "But Dendralon had no idea I would meet you two."

"He sounds like an anti-dandruff shampoo," Craig remarked.

"I'm sorry?" The little fish pushed to the surface.

"It sounds like something Mum would buy," said Craig. "*Dendralon, guaranteed to revitalise limp and lanky hair!*" Craig grinned. "You've got to laugh, haven't you?"

"No you don't," James said. "Not when it's no laughing matter."

Craig's expectant smile slipped into a puzzled frown.

"There is another way," said Mendel. "I could Mind Merge with the dog."

"No you could not!" protested Craig. "I'm not having a half-fish, half-dog pet. And...and I bet it would hurt him too." Both boys looked down into the tin bath in disgust.

"I've got it!" cried James. "What about Mum's brandy barrel?"

"What?" Craig stared incredulously at James. "You're being a numpty again, aren't you?"

"No, I'm not. Dad brought the barrel back from Switzerland – from one of his trips abroad. You know, she actually threw it at him, along with her wedding rings and his coat."

Craig looked over at James. "And you still wonder why your dad beat it?"

James issued a deep sigh. "Bero could wear it round his neck and come with us. Like one of those Saint Bernard dogs."

"And I would be *where*, exactly?" Mendel questioned.

"You'd be inside the barrel, of course, safe and sound." A little smile began to dimple James's cheeks.

This idea wasn't much better than the last, but they decided to give it a try. They found Bero, who tried his best to stand still, and strapped the unwanted gift round his big, furry neck.

Inside his new home – a dull, off-brown, plastic barrel, about four inches in diameter – Mendel tested the walls for leaks. "I suppose it will do," he admitted. There was even a small piece of see-through plastic, embossed with the words, 'Wundadoz Chemicals,' against which he could push a googly eye or flick a golden fin.

At first, his splashing made Bero sniff and cock his crooked ear, but after a few minutes the old dog accepted his new collar and began to wag his tail again.

The boys beamed down at the plastic barrel.

"Well?" said Mendel. "Don't stand there gawping. There's a whole planet at stake here."

"Let's go then," said James.

10

The Loop

Carrying provisions that included a small tub of fish food, a can of flea spray – just in case – and, of course, the blue crystal, James, Craig, Bero, and Mendel passed through the corrugated underpass that led up to Bruce Moor and the Jesus Rocks.

Long ago, some spiritual vandal had painted "Jesus Saves" on the side of the biggest standing stone. Oddly, through the years, someone always refreshed the paint whenever the words faded or became obscured by moss and ferns. It was partly why the Jesus Rocks name had stuck for the five-thousand-year-old, higgledy-piggledy gathering of stones.

Still bathed in summer sunlight, Drumfintley lay spread out below them like a miniature patchwork quilt. The moss-covered houses, the church – missing one gargoyle – and the little green and white village hall were all tinged with an eerie mist drifting up from Loch Echty.

James saw a big, lumbering heron heading towards St. Donan's church spire on its way to the loch. He was sure that this was the second time he'd seen the same bird flying in exactly the same manner. What's more, although they'd been walking for at least an hour, the sun didn't seem to have made much progress across the blue sky. Having dropped closer to the horizon, it was back up; and, although the temperature had cooled, it was now warming again.

"Weird!" James exclaimed. "The spire, look at the church spire! In about two minutes you'll see that big heron twist away from the rectory and veer upward to keep from smacking into the tower. Just watch!"

Craig tracked the heron and sure enough, after about two minutes, it did exactly what James had predicted.

"How did you know that?" asked Craig, bemused.

"Quite simple," answered Mendel. "The Time Loop is now fixed."

James instinctively looked down at the plastic barrel to speak to Mendel. "What do you mean?"

Mendel explained. "When we initiated the time loop, the process set off a reaction that spreads out from the epicentre in the same way ripples do when you throw a pebble into the loch. It's called Nester's Time Loop Paradox."

"You mean the whole world will eventually repeat itself?" asked James, his eyes widening.

"Correct," said Mendel. "The thirty-minute loop will spread outward from Craig's front room until everything repeats at thirty-minute intervals. We are now two minutes into the third loop."

"So it's seventeen minutes past seven again?" James loved puzzles.

"Well done," replied Mendel.

"That poor bird will be knackered," said Craig, always more worried about animals than humans.

"Never mind the heron, what about our mums? All that coffee, and all those biscuits!" James sniggered.

"They're gonna be humongous," laughed Craig, his familiar freckle-faced grin growing ever wider.

"Let's keep moving, boys," said Mendel. "Dendralon knows we're getting close."

"What's the big deal with this Dendralon character?" Craig asked.

And so, with some help from Mendel, James tried his best to explain all about Denthan.

Craig shook his head. "I wouldn't believe any of it, except that I'm already talking to a goldfish."

They had only walked another few paces when James stopped in his tracks. "Wait!" He held up his left hand.

Craig sighed. "What now?"

James bent down and snatched up a hanky-sized piece of green and brown checked velvet cloth from the heather. He rubbed it between his thumb and forefinger before flinging it to the ground as though it had burned him. He stepped back, staring at it.

"It's Dad's lens cleaner for his binoculars," said James.

Craig screwed up his face and rubbed his legs. "How could the police have missed it? I mean, they searched up here for days."

James picked up the lens cleaner again. "I have to go back and tell Mum about this. I have to tell the police!"

"Wait!" Mendel said, concerned. "It could be a trick to delay us. The gateway can only be used at certain times."

"Dad!" James shouted, scanning the horizon until his gaze fixed on the Jesus Rocks. He felt a tinge of fear as he recalled his experience on the moor the day before. However he soon experienced a little flash of elation. Birdsong was everywhere and he could feel the summer breeze on his face. "Maybe Dad's come back," he said.

"James, we have to go now, or it will be too late to save my people. A whole world hangs in the balance." Mendel waited.

"Maybe your dad's gone through the gateway already," suggested Craig.

"Maybe," said James, sceptically. He clutched their green rucksack and eyed the standing stones. "What about the talisman?" he asked Mendel, still not particularly sure what a talisman was.

"A talisman," said Mendel, "is a trinket or charm that is worn round the neck in order to fend off magic. Strong magic. Magic so powerful that it could save or destroy a whole world."

"You've just read my mind again, haven't you?" said James in an accusatory tone.

Craig stared at James blankly. "What was all that about?"

"Apparently," began James, "I'm the only one who can identify some talisman...a trinket or a charm..."

"Yeah, I'm not thick," Craig interrupted, "I heard the explanation."

James held up the lens cloth.

"Not it," said Mendel. "You will know it when you touch the talisman."

Whispering to Craig, James added, "Why am I so special?

"You're special alright," said Craig, sneering again.

"Look, there are monsters...creatures that have already come through the Jesus Rocks. One of them tried to kill us last night."

Craig stayed a little closer to Bero as they made their way across the remaining patch of moor.

Stopping short of the stones, James looked for the footprint and the body of the stoat, but he found nothing to suggest they had ever been there. This ominous disappearance only added to the mystery of the ancient place. With nauseating uneasiness he recalled the crushing despair of the day before.

Bero put his tail between his legs and whined.

Craig knelt to stroke the old dog's head. "There boy, try not to worry. We've got a goldfish to protect us."

The old dog cocked his head and the water in the barrel sloshed to one side. A sliver of gold moved slowly past the plastic window, until a large, disapproving, fishy eye stared up at Craig.

Mendel was not amused.

11

The Gateway

Back at Craig's house, Wee Joe and Helen had now watched the same cartoon episode three times. But in the five minutes before the show would begin they would realise for the third time that the remote control was completely dead – that its two batteries were missing.

While they searched for them, Mufty the hamster would pile more shredded paper on top of the two tube-shaped objects that had magically appeared in her cage the day before.

* * *

High on Bruce Moor, James stepped into the stone circle and ran his hand over the fading graffiti on the largest stone. The painted words were barely visible.

"I'm starving," complained Craig, digging into James's rucksack.

James glared at his friend. "What are you doing?"

"I'm hungry, and so is he!" Craig shook the rucksack in Bero's direction.

"Well, tough luck!" James was still holding his dad's lens cleaner. "Bero can wait!"

Mendel intervened. "We will eat later."

James jerked the rucksack free from Craig then knelt down by Bero.

Just then, a sound distracted James. He slapped his leg and examined a spec of blood before looking up at the sky. "Midges?" he whispered.

Craig followed his gaze.

The sky was black with a moving cloud of insects. They could hear them, droning, louder and louder.

"They are not midges," said Mendel. "Get ready to place the blue crystal where I tell you."

A large moth-like creature landed on Craig's leg and bit him. He slapped it dead and screamed, "Argh! Bloomin' heck, what was that thing?"

"A cleg," said James, pointing down at the squished insect.

"A Zental Moth," corrected Mendel. *"Flipourous invulgaris."* Mendel splashed about and pushed an eye against the window of the brandy barrel.

More and more of the blood-sucking moths dropped into the stone circle and James felt one land on his head. He quickly ruffled his hair and pulled the creature free. It wriggled in his hand. About the size of a butterfly, it had grey wings and a horrible set of white mandibles that clicked together. He shuddered and threw it away.

"Place the crystal at the base of the biggest stone," yelled Mendel.

"They're biting my fingers," complained James.

"Ignore them."

"That's easy for you to say," yelled Craig. "You're safe and sound in a barrel, while we're out here getting eaten alive!"

As more of the Zental Moths pattered down all around them, James shielded his eyes and stumbled towards the biggest standing stone. "I can't see where I'm going!"

"You're fine. Keep walking forward." Mendel sounded calm, but they could tell that he was worried from the way he kept a googly eye pressed against the window of the barrel.

Craig scraped a whole pile of biting moths off Bero as James placed the crystal on the heather at the base of the biggest stone.

"Now turn it North-by-North-East," continued Mendel.

"You mean towards Ben Larvach?" asked James.

"Indeed," agreed Mendel, "but we also need the correct incantation to activate the gateway."

James lowered his gaze and stared down at the hole where Craig had found the blue crystal.

"Bloomin' heck! The cloth!" exclaimed Craig. "It was wrapped in a blue cloth. Would anything have been written on the cloth?" Several more moths battered off of his arms and legs.

"No," said Mendel, "I know the charm."

James screamed as a large moth bit him. As he did, however, another flew straight into his mouth. "Uhhhhhhh tuh tuh..." He bit down hard and the creature burst like a grape, filling his mouth with a sickly sweet pus. He spat again. "It tastes of pear drops."

"I think I'd rather have an actual pear drop!" shouted Craig, taking care to shield his mouth.

Mendel splashed loudly. "Pay attention! Craig, place the crystal on the ground at the base of the biggest stone and point it North by North-West."

"This way?" mumbled Craig, one hand still over his mouth.

"No, the other North by North-West," James scoffed, "towards Ben Larvagh."

Craig looked hurt. "Okay, smarty pants."

James remembered Craig's first day at Drumfintley Primary School, when he'd asked to play football with the local kids. "No chance, Sassenach," had been their reply. Craig's eagerness and upbeat tone had wavered then too.

James felt ashamed.

The moths were finding more and more exposed skin, despite Bero snapping up as many as he could.

Craig twisted the crystal round towards the mountain

at the top of Loch Echty.

"That's it," said Mendel.

"Now what?" yelled Craig. His face was covered in probing insects.

James felt his head pound. He trembled, then said, "Wwwwswarmwwwwkillwww!"

With a rush of air, every insect was gathered up into one massive ball in the sky above their heads before zooming back down the hill and exploding like a firework over the Tank Woods. James watched in awe as a billion wings, feelers and legs all drifted down onto the treetops like snow.

James dropped to his knees, exhausted.

"There. That's better," said Mendel in a self-satisfied tone.

"Why didn't you do that five minutes ago?" moaned Craig.

"I'm still getting used to performing my spells through James. It takes a lot of concentration. Once James finds the talisman it will be so much easier."

"Easier for who?" moaned James. He was still very dizzy, but the pounding in his head was subsiding.

Craig dusted a pile of dead insect wings off his clothes.

"I'm sorry, James," said Mendel, "but I need you to say the charm that will open the gateway."

"Which is?" asked James.

"It's there, written on the rock – 'Jesus Saves'. Only, we read from right to left in Denthan, so it's pronounced, 'sevassusej'. As if it's all one word."

James stared down at the blue crystal in trepidation. The dull pain in his head returned as he uttered the strange charm. He spoke in that strange, fishy way that meant magic was afoot, "Swwewwvwwaaswwuuwwsewwwj!"

At first, nothing happened. Soon, however, the ground began to shake. Within the stone circle, spindly blades of grass began to flutter in a sudden rush of air.

Bero yelped as the turf peeled itself back from the underlying rock with a horrible ripping noise.

They all tried to jump high enough to avoid the sod as it folded, but the sudden movement took their feet away, tipping them forwards.

Where the rock had been, there was now a clear, glass-like sheet that completely filled the middle of the stone circle. Lying on top of it, they remained as still as they could, suspended above an inky black abyss that seemed to stretch into oblivion.

Just as it had the day before, the birdsong stopped and the breeze disappeared. Then, with a loud bang, a thousand hairline cracks began to spread over the surface of the glass.

"Don't anybody move," pleaded James.

Bero, for some unknown reason, seemed to be enjoying himself. His wagging tail slapped hard – *thud, thud, thud* – against the fragile crystal surface.

"Bero! Don't do that," Craig whispered as loud as he dared.

Crack!

The glass beneath them exploded into a fine dust.

They fell, spiralling downwards, head over heels, helpless, unable to breathe, the bright circle of Drumfintley sky above them flashing ever smaller until it disappeared completely.

* * *

As darkness swallowed him, James imagined he was looking down at the gaping hole they'd fallen through, the one in the centre of the Jesus Rocks. The turf was replacing itself as if someone were rolling out a giant carpet. In seconds, nothing looked different. Under the deep blue, umbrella sky, the highland breeze once more flicked trails through the wiry grass. The skylarks sang as they rose into the air then fluttered back down to earth.

Everything was set back in its proper place.

For now.

12

The Caves of Denthan

James was the first to wake. He yawned and rubbed his eyes as they adjusted to a faint glow that seemed to be coming from the sand at his feet. "Where are we, Mendel?" he whispered.

"Not where we should be," answered Mendel, dejectedly. "I think we are in some kind of tunnel system that runs under Denthan, perhaps under the great Forest of Eldane itself. Dendralon must have changed the portal position. This is not where I came through."

Craig winced and rolled onto his elbows. "Dendralon? The shampoo guy again?"

He was about make another stupid comment when James shouted, "Look! Footprints!"

Craig peered down. "Yeah, could be..."

"Dad?" James stood up, the word still echoing along the tunnel system.

Mendel splashed in the barrel. "*Quiet*, James. Denthan is a dangerous place." His golden eye pushed against the plastic window and flicked down at the sandy loam floor. "I'm sorry to disappoint you, James, but I'm sure these are the footprints of *Sygentius trolificus*. Don't you recognise them from the moor?"

"You mean Sleven?" James sighed and placed his foot against the prints. He hadn't noticed the three, long spindly toes. His eyes were still adjusting to the gloomy light. "Yeah, I can see that now." He tried to stifle his disappointment.

"Slever?" Craig said. "Now he sounds as though he's

got a drooling problem."

"His name was *Sleven*," James corrected. "He was a Swamp Troll with size twenty-eight feet and a fondness for squashing stoats."

Craig looked absolutely befuddled.

"But you're not wrong about the drooling bit," James added encouragingly.

Craig still looked bewildered.

"Sleven's dead," clarified Mendel.

Craig knelt down to peer into the little plastic barrel. "How can you be sure that the prints don't belong to James's dad? They might be four or five together in a clump."

Mendel splashed. "Because, Craig, Sleven was a nine-foot-tall Swamp Troll with three toes, not to mention the fact that I am an expert at tracks. I can identify over one million different kinds."

"Alright, alright, but James's dad might have injured himself up there." Craig pointed up at the jagged ceiling. "That grass flipped us right on our faces, you know. It could easily have whipped off a couple of his toes."

Shaking his head at his friend's attempt to defend his reasoning, James kicked the sand until he obliterated the prints.

Mendel responded, "I'm quite sure it was Sleven. It's his master, Dendralon, we need to focus on now. His capacity for evil is unsurpassed, and he will not stop until he saves himself and his Hedra race from certain extinction."

"Great. Can't wait to meet him," drawled Craig.

"So," began James, his words laced with uncertainty, "he wants to save his own kind?"

"Well, yes," said Mendel.

"You can't exactly blame him if—," said James.

"He wants to do it at the expense of every other creature on the planet!" said Mendel.

"Oh," said James. "I see."

"Look boys," continued Mendel, "if we ever become separated, you must find the talisman of Denthan."

"How can we find something if we don't know what it looks like?" asked James.

"You will know, James. It will glow in your hands when you touch it. It will practically sing to you."

Craig issued an ironic 'tut'. "Brilliant. So James has to touch everything he sees until something starts flashing and yodelling at him."

"Don't be so facetious!" snapped Mendel.

Craig drew his head back in surprise. "Sorry, you've got me there. I know it's probably some kind of insult, but—"

"It means, don't be such a Smart Aleck," snapped James. He stared hard at the swaying barrel beneath Bero's chin. "We're not going to get separated anyway, are we?"

Mendel ignored his question and said, "Without the talisman, Denthan is doomed. We are all doomed."

"No pressure then," said Craig, a smile of sorts forming on his lips.

"Why does the talisman matter so much?" asked James, intrigued to know how important his unwanted task actually was.

"The talisman has the power to stop Dendralon from carrying out his plan. I was banished to your world because he knew that I could find it – that its magic would be drawn to mine in a time of great need. It can override his dark magic, if used correctly. He is determined that only his race, the Hedra, will survive the downfall of Denthan."

"Wait a minute," said Craig, his expression hardening, "are you telling me that we've just arrived in a world that is about to disappear?"

"All worlds disappear eventually," said Mendel.

Craig scowled. "How long have we got?"

"Hopefully," began Mendel, "we will have long enough to retrieve the talisman, stop Dendralon, and find James's father."

James sighed deeply before trudging down the tunnel after Bero and the little swaying barrel.

"Tell me more about Dendralon," said Craig, staggering onward. "What's a Hedra?"

"The Hedra are a race of reptilians that evolved, without interruption, from the early Saurs of Denthan," Mendel explained.

"*Saurs*? As in dino...?" asked Craig, really starting to regret his involvement in this whole weird escapade.

"That's correct. But whereas your world experienced their global extinction sixty-five million years ago, ours did not." Mendel's voice deepened. "If we can find the talisman in time, there's also a good chance that I will regain the full extent of my powers...and save my people."

"And all the other creatures that live here too," suggested Craig.

"Quite," said Mendel.

James paused. Mendel's reply to Craig's question had been a little less convincing than he would have liked.

"There is, however," continued Mendel, "only one place in the whole of Denthan where I can reverse this metamorphosis and regain my own form."

"Where's that?" asked James.

Mendel splashed some more, causing Bero to twitch his ears. "At the sacred Eden Tree on an island called Senegral, in the Forest of Eldane. If we ever get separated, you must meet me there."

James's eyes widened. "I wish you'd stop talking about us becoming separated. I thought you were going to look after us." He scanned the dark tunnel ahead and increased his pace.

"I have every intention of doing so, but..."

"But what?" asked Craig, anxiously looking back into the gloom.

"It's better to be safe than sorry," said Mendel. "Always have a plan B."

As they shuffled along in the darkness, the dank roof dripped water onto their hair and clothes. The smell in the tunnel reminded James of old churches – damp horsehair and musty pews, with just a hint of woodworm.

"Which way now?" James asked, seeing a labyrinth of caves and tunnels stretching ahead of them.

"Follow the dog," Mendel told him.

The boys weren't convinced that Bero would really know where to go either. But they followed the old mutt anyway, through high-roofed chambers as big as cathedrals and through tiny, little corridors that made their footsteps echo until the sound blended into one long clatter. Finally, after much crouching and scraping of skin, they stood up to find themselves in an inconceivably enormous cavern.

Craig cricked his neck as he tried to pick out the ceiling. "You could fit the whole of Drumfintley in here."

"And most of Loch Echty," added James, staring in awe.

Behind the fearless Bero, the boys walked quite a distance into the chamber before noticing a gigantic wooden door ahead of them that appeared to be glowing even brighter than the sand. Flanked by two oversized torches, it stood at least fifty feet high.

As they stared up at the door, they felt the pull of the light drawing them nearer and nearer.

"It's a door!" Craig hissed.

"Duh. You think?" James muttered irritably. He hated it when Craig stated the obvious: *it's a lovely day; that's a big tree; it's raining outside.* James wanted to shout, 'Of course it's a door!' Instead he said, "Can you feel that?" He searched for words to describe the magnetic pull of the strange amber light. "The way it's drawing us closer?"

Craig reached out for something to hold onto. "Yeah, I can't stop my legs! I don't like this one bit. Mendel, what's happening?"

"Keep up," Mendel dictated. "I think I know where we are."

Something in Mendel's voice told James that the wizard was concerned.

The boys did as they were told, but soon stopped to gape at a huge statue. The stone creature leered down at them with a malevolent frown. Positioned in a recess next to the giant door, it was almost hidden from sight. Its horned head, James decided, was either a bull or buffalo. He could just make out a pair of beady eyes, barely visible beneath a deeply furrowed brow.

"What is that thing?" whispered Craig, gazing dreamily at the effigy.

"Is it a man or a giant?" whispered James.

"It is *Homo minatorres*, known in the legends of your world as the Minotaur," answered Mendel.

"Looks nothing like a Minotaur," said Craig. "This one's all hairy, and its head looks more like a pig with horns than a—"

"I can assure you," interrupted Mendel, "that it *is* a Minotaur! A distant relation of yours, in fact."

James tittered. "Look Craig, it's got your ears."

"Hardee-har-har!" Suddenly self-conscious, Craig pawed at a large freckled lug.

Mendel once again ignored them. "They were wiped out along with the Neanderthals and many other sub-species. It was branded a monster and destroyed."

"I can understand the monster bit," James said. He reached out and touched the ugly, stone creature. As he did, however, the strange amber light that had drawn them to the door disappeared.

"Why did you touch it?" cried Mendel, in a high,

exasperated voice.

"Why not?" James yelped, startled.

"Always, always ask if it's safe first." Mendel sounded like he was biting his fishy lip in an effort to control his anger.

"And was it?" Craig wondered aloud.

"Was it *what*?" demanded Mendel.

James looked back at his freckle-faced friend as he rephrased the question.

"Was it safe to touch the Minotaur?" asked Craig.

Creeaak!

"There's your answer!" Mendel snapped, his voice barely audible above the deafening noise that now filled the cave. The huge door's ancient iron braces strained as it was pried open by an ominous force. Almost immediately, the air switched from smelling like an old church, to stinking like a used toilet.

Frozen to the spot, they stared as several bands of iron buckled away from the ancient wood.

"Through the door," Mendel ordered. "Now!"

Cracks and bangs echoed round the big chamber like explosions.

For a split second the boys could only stand terrified, gagging at the unbearable smell, but when they saw Bero bounding forward, they dashed after him.

"Don't leave us!" yelled James. Surprised to find his breathing regular and controlled, James felt a rush of energy and power – a power he hadn't felt since Mendel's spell had opened his airways that morning. Despite his fear, he revelled in a feeling of freedom; freedom from the ever-present weight on his chest that had stifled him in Drumfintley.

"I can breathe..." he shouted after Craig and Bero. "I can breathe here!"

"Maybe not for much longer!" Craig yelled back.

Heavy footsteps closed behind them as Craig reached back and tugged at James's shirt, pulling him onwards.

The stench grew worse as they raced round a corner only to skid to a halt. They had come to a dead-end: a solid wall with three doors set into it.

"Now what?" blurted James.

"Go through the middle one!" snapped Mendel.

Bang-slide-crunch. Bang-slide-crunch.

Stone on stone. Something extremely big was moving along the tunnel behind them.

"Open the middle door!" yelled Mendel.

They both pushed against it as hard as they could.

"It won't budge," gasped James. His fear hung in the stale air like treacle, slowing him down and cluttering his thoughts.

Bero barked.

They tried again, and this time Bero joined in, putting his full weight against the heavy middle door. As his big paws scratched the grey wood, he panted and yelped.

At last, the door began to move, but only as a shadow filled the tunnel behind them. Two horns stretched along the wall, followed by the distorted silhouette of a bulky body, a jagged club lifted high above its head.

Horrified, they stared along the tunnel until, massive and lumbering, the Minotaur came into view.

It snorted loudly, its wide, dripping nostrils flaring. More stone than flesh, it leered at them with black, piggy eyes.

Seeing the beast so close behind, James felt his legs turn to jelly as his remaining strength ebbed away.

"It can't see us," whispered Mendel, "but it can hear your steps and smell your breath."

The boys gave each other a wide-eyed look then immediately covered their mouths, wishing they had cleaned their teeth more thoroughly.

"One last push!" shouted Mendel.

Ignoring their aches and pains, the two boys slammed their backs against the door and pushed with their legs.

There was a loud crack as the door swung open. They all fell through, spilling onto the floor on the other side.

Thump!

The door slammed shut behind them.

"Yes!" panted James. "We did it." He shut his eyes, but the goldfish-wizard's voice seared through his body like electricity.

"Get up!" shouted Mendel. "Keep running!"

As James and Craig hauled themselves forward again, the door behind them burst into a thousand pieces, and a giant club appeared through the flurry of wooden splinters.

13

The Door to Denthan

Bero took the lead, all of them racing round corners until they arrived at a seemingly endless set of stone steps. Without looking back, they leapt up them two at a time, until the boys began to overtake Bero.

"He's not so good on stairs anymore," Craig panted.

James could see Bero's back legs wobbling.

"Uurrgghhuu!" the Minotaur bellowed up at them and smacked its club down hard on the bottom steps.

Standing about twenty yards beneath them, the monster moved awkwardly as it attempted to place its oversized, stone feet on the ancient stairway. Growing impatient, it shifted its weight, brought the club back behind its head, and threw it.

Whistling up the stairs like a cannonball, the club smashed into the ceiling above them, sending a storm of shattered stalactites down upon their heads.

James leapt aside as the debris rained all around. Through the crashing of falling stones, he heard Bero howling woefully.

And then all went quiet.

Dust hung in the air like a thick, grey curtain, choking and blinding him at the same time. James coughed. "Craig...?"

The Minotaur immediately roared at the sound of his voice. "Uurrgghhuu!"

"Bero?" James's voice was thin and wistful. His heart pounded hard. Somewhere in the confusion, not too far below them, he could hear the Minotaur moving. He heard

Craig call out too, "Bero!" But there was still no sign of the old dog, nor of Mendel.

James rubbed his eyes and shook his hair free of stones and muck. "Craig, come on!" His best friend was only a few yards away.

Bang! Bang! Bang!

Closer than before, the huge stone beast shifted below them.

James groped for Craig's arm. "Move further up. It's crawling towards us. Look!"

Through the dust and fallen rock, they could make out the Minotaur struggling forward. Although it looked like a mass of moving stone, it stank like rotting flesh. James winced as the acrid stench caught in his throat. Yellow liquid dripped from the monster's flaring nostrils and splashed onto the steps.

Desperately, the boys peered behind the beast for any sign of Bero, but their hearts sank when they saw the great piles of heavy stone that littered the stairs.

James clawed at Craig's grey jumper. "I can see a door above us. Come on!"

Craig held back.

"Craig, for Pete's sake!" snapped James.

"Yes, but Bero!" Craig looked as if he was about to give up.

James found Craig's hand this time and yanked him up the stairs.

"Faster!" James cried as the Minotaur's giant hand slammed down, right where Craig had stood moments before.

Fifty yards on they reached a door and pushed it as hard as they could.

It held fast.

"It's hopeless." Craig slumped against a damp, stone wall.

"Get up!" James shouted, taking over. He looked around and saw something that resembled the font in St Donan's church. He peered into the still water. "A key!" He pushed his hand in and let out a scream. "Awch! It's boiling hot. I... I can't reach it." James shoved his hand into his armpit, gripping his throbbing fingers tightly with his upper arm.

The Minotaur's snorts and bangs were almost upon them again.

Thinking quickly, James pulled a chunk of damp, brown moss from the wall and wrapped it round his hand. As he turned, about to try for the key again, he hesitated. Two letters had been carved into the back of the door: D. P.

"Craig, look! D.P. David Peck. Dad must have been through here, too!"

"It could be Dimple Pukepants for all you know," his friend grumbled. Craig glanced nervously back and forth between the letters on the wall and the Minotaur.

This time James plunged his hand even deeper into the well, pushing the pain to the back of his mind.

"Got it!" he shouted triumphantly, brandishing his prize.

The Minotaur was within six feet of the boys and roared as James tried to push home the strange bronze key and turn it in the lock.

With a loud click the door flew open and a current of air sucked them through.

Blinded by an incredible brightness ahead, they stumbled forward, shielding their eyes from the glare.

Bang!

As if being blinded wasn't bad enough, the explosion above their heads was deafening. James was thrown to the ground, his senses numbed.

14

The Quetza

James rolled over, still protecting his eyes, and bumped into Craig.

"I can't see!" Craig sobbed.

"Me neither," gasped James. He tried to open his eyes a little more and found they were gradually acclimatising to the new light. He was aware of a yellow cloud of dust descending on them. A moss-covered door lay open behind them. A trail of dirt and debris disappeared into the blackness beyond. Small tear tracks ran over Craig's fingers and down his cheeks like little streams.

"Where's the Minotaur?" Craig demanded.

James found his friend's arm and pulled him close. "I'm not sure," he whispered, "I think it exploded right over us. This dust...it's all that's left." He shielded his eyes and stared back at the door. "Where's Bero?"

Craig shook his head, his eyes half open. "He has to be there. He can't be... Bero!"

As James looked around for the dog, his attention was drawn to the landscape ahead of them. Glancing up at the sky he took in a sharp breath. "Craig...Craig, look!"

"What?"

"There are two suns!" James tried to stand. He wasn't sure if he was seeing things right.

"Of course there are two suns," said a voice. "This is Denthan."

The two boys nearly jumped out of their skins.

"Bero!" They both shouted with joy as, out of the dust and darkness, the old Golden Retriever plodded towards them, his little plastic barrel still intact and his feathered tail thrashing behind him in a display of utter delight.

"The Minotaur stepped right over us," explained Mendel. "And who, if you don't mind me asking, is Dimple Pukepants?"

Still half blinded by dust and tears, Craig laughed and crawled towards Bero.

"There was a DP carved into the door," said James. "My dad's left his initials as a clue!" He pushed Craig to the side and knelt down beside the barrel. "It's just the kind of thing he would do. Tell him, Mendel. Tell Craig that's what it will be!"

"Look, James," said Mendel, "the initials could also stand for Dendralon Pendragon. "I'm not saying it *wasn't* your dad," he added hastily, "I just think we should consider all the options before jumping to conclusions."

James slumped down and sighed in despair.

Craig shook more Minotaur fragments from his hair. "Why would the grand master of evil, or whatever he is, take time out to scratch his initials on a bit of old rock? You'd think he had better things to do."

"When a wizard carves his initials by a doorway or near a ford," said Mendel, "it is a sign that he has set magic in motion to guard that spot. This was a case in point. Don't you see James, that if you hadn't opened the door in time...?"

"You mean you didn't do any magic to protect us?" asked James, stunned.

"Sorry," began Mendel, "but coming through a gateway to another world is quite a draining experience. Besides, there's nothing wrong with getting a bit of luck now and again."

"Luck?" echoed Craig.

"You see, Minotaurs cannot exist in daylight. They are obliterated by the slightest hint of sunlight." Mendel's golden fin flickered past the window of the barrel as he somersaulted inside. "Oh, it's so good to be back home in Denthan!"

James could almost hear a smile in Mendel's voice.

Brushing themselves down, they stared, once again, at the breathtaking views before them. The two suns threw a wondrous light over a beautiful land. Blue mountains rose in the distance, higher than any James had ever imagined, and an immense forest, filled with peculiar trees and vines, stretched as far as they could see.

* * *

It was Trinity Sunday and the twenty-four hour clock on the crusty-brown oven had just clicked to 19:15. Father Michael was having a bad day. Things were not going well, not well at all. Having taken his position as Priest-in-Charge only nine months earlier, he was struggling with depressingly low attendances at the eleven o'clock service and an increasing mountain of paperwork in his study. But the worst of it was his flock. They were always suspicious, always thinking the worst.

Everyone in Drumfintley seemed to have a massive chip on their shoulder and it was wearing him down. In his sermons he had made clear that it was much better to be positive about others – to think well of your fellow man. But so far there was nothing to suggest that his congregation was listening.

He thought he might go for a walk to clear his head. Perhaps he could regain his confidence through some spiritual contemplation, something he desperately needed after the incident with Cathy Peck's son, James.

He winced with humiliation at the recollection of being kicked in the unmentionables in front of Cathy Peck (and, he was sure, a curtain-twitching Ephie Blake). He had startled the boy, but why had the little rotter—?

Clang!

Michael nearly jumped out of his skin. "What the heck! Mr MacNulty?"

"Ywes Favar." The voice drifted in through the open kitchen window.

Michael leaned out. "What's that noise...and why are you talking like that?"

"Twalking wike what?" Mr MacNulty was rummaging through some old bikes and bells in Michael's garden shed.

"Twalking – I mean, *talking* – like *that*?" replied Michael.

"I cwanny fwind ma teef!" MacNulty struggled to stay on his feet as Patch, Michael's Jack Russell pup, jumped round him in little circles, barking excitedly.

"Patch! Come here! Leave Mr MacNulty alone." The little black and white pup did a half twist in mid-air, then latched her teeth onto the sleeve of MacNulty's tweed jacket.

"Patch, stop that!" scolded Michael. But the reprimand went unheeded as all three of them became distracted by a large, grey heron flying overhead. Disturbed by the commotion below, the bird corrected its flight, soaring just ten or so feet above their heads and only narrowly missing the church tower as it flapped onward. Watching its antics, both Michael and MacNulty noticed at the same time that something was missing from the top of the west-facing parapet.

"Fwamin' vwandwals!" MacNulty ranted, enunciating as best he could.

Michael looked round, shielding his eyes against the evening sun, then stared back up at the tower in disbelief. "What kind of vandals would steal a half-ton gargoyle from a fifty foot tower? They'd need a helicopter."

As MacNulty leaned back, straining to see the swooping heron, Patch made one last ardent tug and sent him tumbling backwards into a pile of old paint pots.

Clatter! Bang!

"Oow!" An old paintbrush, with solid white bristles, ricocheted off his balding head.

Patch, seemly satisfied, released her grip and scampered back up the garden.

Once hidden in the rose bed, the little dog resumed gnawing on poor old MacNulty's false teeth.

* * *

James, the green rucksack between his knees, produced his dad's checked lens cleaner. He teased it between his fingers. He could never let something rest once he'd set his mind on it. "You can both believe what you want," he muttered, half to himself, "but I know my dad's been here. I just know it. If I do anything here worthwhile, it will be to prove you wrong on that score."

"If you don't find the talisman you won't be able to prove anything, you stupid boy."

James frowned at the barrel. "You know, sometimes I could…"

"Stupid boy," echoed Craig, his familiar grin fixed firmly back on his face.

James felt the anger rise in his chest but it subsided as he stared round in disbelief. Denthan was so different, so unusual.

Craig was soon busy checking Bero's back legs for any damage he may have suffered in the Minotaur's tunnel, and Mendel looked to be getting his bearings. With a swish of his fishy tail, the wizard-goldfish headed for his plastic window.

"Where now?" asked James, still irritated by the 'stupid

boy' comments.

"Well," Mendel pondered, "I believe we should walk into the trees ahead and look for the path that bears south."

Ahead of them, the strange forest seemed to go on forever. Long, mossy strands covered the trees, with only the occasional palm-sized leaf poking through the dense covering. It looked impenetrable.

Where they were sitting, close to the top of a small valley, there was little or no shade. The twin suns seemed to cancel out each other's shadows, filling the place with a strange, unfaltering light.

"It's just like the kind of light you get on stage," said Craig. "Remember, James? Like the pantomime last Christmas, when you forgot your lines."

"Mmm..." James mused, looking round. Where they sat, the vegetation was sparse and the grass woody and tough.

Behind them, the moss-covered door had disappeared. There was no sign of the black opening in the cliff, or, for that matter, the yellow Minotaur dust.

As the boys' eyes adjusted more fully to the light, they began to see all sorts of creatures around them. The first ones they noticed were funny bird-like animals jumping from bush to bush. Resembling small geese with enlarged beaks, they sported red-feathered, vestigial wings that flicked and fluttered as they clumsily hopped across the ground on ungainly legs.

"Dodos?" wondered Craig. He blinked uncertainly at James. "They kinda look like the ones in your *Extinction With Distinction* book." He turned to the little barrel. "They aren't dangerous, are they?"

One of the creatures bounced a little closer.

"Not particularly," said Mendel. "You are looking at a Quezta, *Queztala invigouralis*. In fact, it shares the same gene tree as your Dodo. But this variety managed to survive and become more successful due to its unique defence mechanism."

"Which is?" James queried.

"Which is to spit Penturic acid at any attacker," said Mendel. "As long as you don't make any aggressive movements, you should be fine."

"I thought you said they were harmless," accused Craig, inadvertently inhaling a floating clump of Bero's fur as he petted the dog's coat. "Phe, phe..." Craig choked, then coughed out a yellow fur ball from between his teeth.

The little dodo-like Quezta, along with several of its inquisitive friends, jerked upright. The one nearest Craig turned its head to get a better look.

"You stupid boy!" Mendel scolded.

Yes! This time it's Craig's turn for a telling off, thought James.

"I only coughed, for goodness sake!" protested Craig.

Immediately, four or five Quezta surrounded him. The nearest one, standing only a couple of steps away, spat a jet of green liquid into the air.

Both boys jumped to their feet.

Mendel splashed inside the barrel. "Watch out for that acid! It'll burn straight through you!"

Craig and James leapt this way and that as the Quezta shot more green jets at them from several directions.

"Whatever you do, don't run," Mendel warned. "Just walk calmly towards the forest."

"That's easy for you to say," snapped Craig, still darting about. "That one just missed my leg."

"Walk!" Mendel's normally rich voice had risen an octave, making him sound like an over-anxious parent.

James struggled to keep himself from running off in a mad panic. A splash of acid landed near his foot and he ended up stumbling the last few yards to the edge of the forest, hoping all the while that the birds wouldn't give chase.

At last, when they got far enough from the Quezta to feel safe, they stopped and looked back. One of awkward-looking birds, which had been unfortunate enough to get acid sprayed over its back in the mêlée, was now the subject of the other birds' interest.

"Yuk! Look at that poor thing," said Craig, scrunching up his eyes. "It's melted."

"Poor wee thing, my ear," scoffed James. "That could have been one of us." He was about to chastise Craig for starting the trouble in the first place, but decided not to bother. Mendel was doing enough of that already. He was showing his true colours now that he was back on home turf. The wizard-goldfish was certainly less patient.

Mendel advised that they put some distance between themselves and the 'harmless' Quezta, so they kept walking for another hour. Unable to see any sign of a path at first, they had to clamber and squeeze through the undergrowth for almost a mile. Despite their struggle, James continued to be amazed that he could breathe so freely in the Denthan air.

"There!" Mendel's triumphant voice filled their heads as they broke through a thick patch of mossy vine, "The path to Gwendral."

"To where?" enquired James.

"Gwendral; the magical city that holds the key to our survival." Mendel sounded excited. They heard him splashing about beneath Bero's chin.

"But I thought you said that the talisman holds the key to our survival?" said James.

"And that Eden Tree you talked about," added Craig.

"Stop for a moment, and I'll tell you more."

The boys were exhausted and gladly sat down on a nearby log.

"Don't get me wrong," said James, "I'm tired and I want to rest, but I thought you said that we had to get the talisman first?"

"That's right, James, but a little clarification might be expedient at this stage."

"Expedi-what?" queried Craig.

"Worthwhile," explained Mendel. "Can you see the large circle of red on the Eastern horizon?"

The boys nodded.

"That's Tealfirth, the larger of our two suns." Mendel sounded sad. "I'm afraid it's dying."

"But you've got one spare," said Craig, pointing to the smaller sun setting in the West.

Mendel puh-puhed against the plastic window of his barrel. "I have studied supernovas in other galaxies, and my calculations tell me that Denthan will not survive. We will have to use the city to rescue as many as we can before that happens."

James frowned. "How can a city rescue you from a world that's going to explode?"

"Gwendral is a huge gateway," Mendel told him. "All those who are inside the city walls could be saved by being transported to another world."

"You mean," said James, "it's like a huge ark?"

"So that's why Dendralon wants to take control of it!" exclaimed Craig.

"Exactly!" exclaimed Mendel. "But there are a few other issues to resolve apart from changing back into my own form and convincing my people that King Athelstone is, in fact, the impostor Dendralon."

"What would they be, then..." pressed Craig, teasing Bero's fur, "these 'other issues'?"

Mendel cleared his throat. "Well, once we find the talisman, we also need to get hold of three unique crystals so that we can turn the city into a functioning gateway. Without the talisman these crystals are no more than lumps of rock, but with it..."

"The crystals turn the city into an ark?" said James.

"Good boy," said Mendel.

"I thought you said we were 'stupid'," said Craig. "Make up your mind."

Mendel cleared his throat with a bubbly cough and continued. "Each of the three ancient races have a crystal: the Salt Trolls, the Osgrunfs and the Hedra."

The boys looked confused.

"They are the three most ancient races besides the Manimals, and—"

"Hold the bus!" cried Craig. "We know Dendralon's one of these reptile Hedra things, but what the heck are 'Manimals'?"

Mendel laughed. "I am one. But that doesn't really help, does it?"

The boys stared down at the golden blob inside the brandy barrel.

"Not really," said Craig.

"We look a bit like you, Craig."

"Poor things." James shook his head in sympathy.

"Hardee-har-har," grumbled Craig.

"But with some modifications," Mendel interjected.

"Modifications?" echoed James.

"Well, due to the brightness of our suns, our eyes are different from yours – they are slit like a cat's and mostly white. Other than that, we evolved from similar creatures and so are anatomically very similar."

"Ooo, scary!" said Craig. "So, all these things you have to do…why can't you do them as a goldfish? Find the talisman, get the crystals, defeat Dendralon…"

"I'm simply not as powerful in this form. I can perform my magic much more effectively as a Manimal. And to defeat Dendralon, I will need to perform the most powerful magic I can muster."

James was concerned. "So you really need us, don't you?"

"Of course I do. I wouldn't be here right now if it wasn't for you two. I'd still be in a bin or..."

"Or you'd be gobbled up like a fish finger," said Craig.

"Quite," said Mendel.

"And how long have we got?"

"To do all three? I'm not sure. A week, a month, a day..."

"A *day*? Well, that's just fantastic, isn't it?" James slumped off the moss-covered log and onto the ground. "And you've forgotten about number four."

"Number four?" Mendel repeated.

"Your number four, but *my* number one," James sighed. "I need to find and rescue my dad before this world blows to smithereens."

Mendel sighed, "Ah, of course."

15

The Talisman and the King

Craig shook his head in an aloof way that made James want to punch him on the nose.

"What?" asked James, trying his best to stay calm.

"You don't even know if your dad is here," pressed Craig.

Mendel's voice was sharp. "No need to start all that again. Let's move on. We have a talisman to find. We need to quicken our pace."

"Oh, come on," whined Craig. "Bero needs a drink, and I'm exhausted."

Mendel released a stream of bubbles. "But it's only ten more miles to the Eden Tree."

"*Ten*?" wailed Craig.

James stopped and stared down at the brandy barrel. "So, you expect me to find the talisman in this forest? In Eldane? Between here and the Eden Tree?"

"That's what the ancient scrolls say." Mendel eased away from his plastic window.

"What ancient scrolls?" asked James.

"I have read thousands of books and manuscripts over the years, and one in particular, The Scroll of the Twin Suns, says the talisman will only appear when Denthan is near to destruction."

"What else does it say?" asked Craig.

Mendel sighed. "It says that the talisman will appear to someone from another world. It says that Manimal magic will attract it but…" Mendel seemed to be deep in thought before he said, "*The talisman moves through ancient leaves and yet, at times, stands still. No Denthan eyes can see it; some say they never will.*"

James gawped at Craig for a moment. His best friend looked tired and scared. "So can we stop and rest or not?"

Mendel appeared at the window of the barrel. "Fine, fine. I suppose it'll be dark soon," he relented. "We should be relatively safe here."

"You don't sound too sure about that," said James. He almost split his face in two with a huge yawn before glancing down at his dad's lens cloth. He still had it, clutched tight, in his right hand.

As they explored their camp, the twin suns still winked through the mossy hue that laced the barren branches above their heads. James noticed that the larger sun, Tealfirth, seemed to pulse like an angry wound.

It wasn't too cold, so when the boys found a small stream for Bero they splashed each other with the clear water, realising that they didn't have to wash, or even brush their teeth.

"It feels like we've been running and screaming non-stop since we left my bedroom," James remarked with a weak smile.

"We have," said Craig, grinning as he turned his attention to Bero and Mendel. "Are you absolutely sure we're safe here?"

"The woods don't seem very welcoming," added James.

Bero gave him a quizzical look, and there was no reply from Mendel, so they opened the green rucksack and rummaged about.

"Mmm…" James produced two Caramel Logs, and they munched on them, wondering whether Mendel was just sleeping or in a huff at their refusal to go any further. They drank their juice, ignored the apples, and shared a piece of cold chicken with Bero. James sprinkled some fish food into the barrel and looked down at the goldfish that had taken them so far from home.

"I miss my mum," said Craig as he snuggled into Bero.

"I miss mine, too," sighed James.

Craig shot James a puzzled glance. "But she's always shouting and screaming at you."

"Yeah, I know. But I still miss her." James felt weird defending his mum. He could hear her now in his head: "If you would just behave yourself and keep your room tidy, I wouldn't *have* to shout all the time!"

James looked across at Craig and felt a pang of jealousy. His best pal had a dog to cuddle, and a dad, even if he was in the navy and a mile under the Arctic Circle.

As the suns set and the forest darkened, a tremendous racket filled the evening air: grunts, squeaks, growls, and a blood-curdling wail in the distance that sounded as if something was being eaten alive. The boys shuffled closer to each other.

James prayed nothing would appear out of the dim light between the trees. After an hour, when nothing had, the din became part of the background noise.

Half asleep, James closed his eyes and imagined his dad climbing over roots and leaping across streams, just as they had done. He didn't have a wizard to protect him or even explain what was going on. And then James opened his eyes with a start. He'd seen the expression on his dad's face. He'd looked...content. Not tired or terrified, but content. As if he was pleased to be somewhere else, away from his screaming wife and the rest of his life in Drumfintley.

"Are you okay?" said Craig. "You look annoyed."

"Of course, I'm annoyed," snapped James. "We're stuck in a nightmare."

* * *

High in the citadel, on a balcony that led off from the main Council Chamber, Cimerato, a young captain in full armour, looked out over the colourful buildings below. The city of Gwendral, bathed in fading sunlight, shone pink and gold above the treetops of Eldane. Each of its spires, studded with glittering gems, stretched high above the cobbled streets.

In the distance, tiny flying reptiles could be seen spinning down over the rooftops, while fragile plumes of chimney smoke sailed skyward, only to dissolve in the evening breeze.

It was still warm in the purple glow of the two suns. The larger, Tealfirth, sunk slowly behind the jagged peaks of the far off mountains to the east of the city. To the west, the smaller sun, Zalion, had almost reached the surface of the Gorton Sea, its reflection shimmering on the still waters. Both suns would set at the same time, and both would rise on opposite horizons nine hours later.

In the Council Chamber behind Cimerato, discussions about the reptilian Hedra, who normally lived in the southern marshes, were in full flow.

The captain reluctantly stepped in from the balcony just in time to see his father, Lord Eldane, enter the room and step forward into a semicircle of stone scales that fanned outward to the Chamber. There, he directed his speech to the Council members who occupied the ornate wooden seats facing him. Behind him was an ivory throne on which the tall, black-robed figure of King Athelstone sat observing the proceedings, tapping a gnarled stick on the floor and fidgeting distractedly.

"They have gathered by the thousands, I'm told," said Lord Eldane, "and are only two days away, or less. They have Raptors and siege weapons." He cleared his throat, then continued, "We have not had to defend our beautiful city for more than a hundred years and we have to ask ourselves: are we ready?" His disquieting words echoed round the Chamber, filling its lofty ceilings and serpentine carvings.

While Lord Eldane had spoken strongly and clearly, there was a trace of wariness in his voice as he turned to face King Athelstone. "My son, Cimerato, has seen all this with his own eyes."

On hearing this, Cimerato walked into the main Chamber and made his way to the throne. The still-handsome King Athelstone eyed the young man to whom he'd entrusted the preparation of the defences.

"Please carry on, Father," said Cimerato, bowing briefly to his King before sitting down. Almost six feet tall, his muscles tensed beneath his yellow armour as he placed the tip of his curved sword on the floor. He rested his hands round the leather hilt and took in the scene.

Athelstone shifted on his throne, his long black hair framing his face. He scratched the skin on his forearm, then stood. He, too, was an imposing figure, taller even than Cimerato.

"I think your father has said enough, Cimerato." He grasped Lord Eldane's shoulder, causing the old man to wince. Athelstone glanced over to see Cimerato's reaction and smiled at what he saw. "We are running out of time, and the Hedra are at least fifty thousand strong!"

"We still have time!" proclaimed one of the younger councillors. He stood up and bravely faced King Athelstone. Cimerato watched Athelstone's eyes bore into the young councillor and knew what would happen next. The poor man promptly shut his mouth and sat down heavily in his seat, his young face pale and wizened. Cimerato wasn't the only one to regret the day they'd welcomed their lost king back into Gwendral and he felt his frustration build as he saw the whole Council now try to avoid Athelstone's gaze.

Cimerato recalled how King Athelstone had blamed Mendel for the evils that now plagued Gwendral, and how, little by little, he'd turned the main families against the wizard. When Mendel in return had claimed the King was an impostor, Cimerato had known something would have to be done. They could not execute the old wizard – he had helped his people for too long – but finally the Council had agreed to banish Mendel from Denthan, sending him through one of his own gateways in a form that would prevent him from using his magic.

Strangely, ever since Mendel's banishment, sightings of Tree Trolls and Centides – the giant predatory insects that inhabited the darkest parts of the Forest of Eldane – had increased. This had caused panic. Most of the city blamed the Council for having been too hasty in its decision to cast out Mendel. And now, with a great army of Hedra massing to the south, the city's future looked grim.

It all seemed very odd, very suspicious. Worse, the Council seemed unsure what to do. Its members missed Mendel's leadership and wisdom.

Although Athelstone still looked as strong and as fit as the day he'd disappeared, there was something about him that wasn't quite right. A few were even suggesting that perhaps Mendel had been correct about the King. Before, Athelstone had been a calm and wise leader; he was now prone to violent mood swings. Indeed, more and more often he would hiss with rage when dissenters dared to cross him. Today was no exception, for as Athelstone set his strange stare on Cimerato, he cracked his gnarled staff against the scaled floor and said, "Come closer, Cimerato, Son of Eldane."

Cimerato had been told of Athelstone's announcement in advance and dreaded the Council's reaction to the news.

Cimerato joined his father on the scaled semicircle that fanned out from the throne. The Councillors began to murmur, and shuffled nervously in their seats, but all sound and movement ceased when Athelstone fixed his cold gaze on them.

The King began, "The Osgrunfs have been seen in the east, gathered in a great herd that stretches back far into the Forest of Eldane. To the west, the Gorton Sea bubbles with Salteths and Salt Trolls."

Mumbles and mutterings once again filled the grand Council Chamber.

Athelstone walked to the edge of the floor's scaled semicircle and raised both hands. "In the light of this and the massive Hedra army gathering to the south, I have reluctantly decided that the complete evacuation of the city is our only option. We must leave Gwendral."

Everyone stared at the King in disbelief.

Cimerato's father, Lord Eldane, was visibly shaken. "I know we discussed this privately, but we can't just abandon our city to the hordes..."

Athelstone's Manimal eyes, white, with a single vertical pupil, flashed with a sudden fury.

"We have no choice, Lord Eldane." Athelstone ground out the words impatiently as he stepped past the old man and his son to address the Councillors more directly. "Hedra, Osgrunfs and Salt Trolls, all marching this way. My information is that they are determined to take Gwendral. All because of Mendel's ridiculous prophecies. We cannot defend ourselves properly with only three thousand soldiers to protect the city walls. Think of the women and children. We must keep them safe." He paused. "I can tell that you are not happy about this, but there is little choice. We can either welcome the idea of living in a new city or sit here and wait to be slaughtered. I have already instructed my soldiers to open the secret tunnels to Nordengate. We should use them now if we want to survive."

When Cimerato saw the look of utter despair on his father's face, he knew that he too would have to challenge the King. Abandoning their great city was unthinkable. Knowing that he was possibly putting his life at risk, he stepped forward to address the Council...

16

Eethan

Having admitted defeat in the hunt for the remote control's batteries, the women resumed their conversation in Jean's living room.

"Not in our school, not in Drumfintley!" Cathy Peck declared passionately. She was onto her favourite subject: the downward spiral of standards at the local school. "If we get the city intake here, I'm sending James off to Balfinty instead. Drumfintley's had it. The place is going to be overrun by bullies and thugs—"

"And that's just the teachers!" Jean finished, biting her bottom lip to suppress a smile. She quickly changed the subject. "I meant to thank David for getting me the hamster for Wee Joe's birthday."

"Mmm..." Cathy's frown became more pronounced.

Bang!

A deafening thud shook the thin ceiling above their heads and a shower of dust drifted onto their glasses.

"Helen?" Jean immediately stood up.

"Now what? Why is it, any time I'm on the phone or with visitors, they decide to wreck the place?"

* * *

Upstairs, Wee Joe had dislodged the bowling ball from the top shelf of his big brother's cupboard while trying to find a game. A piece of blue cloth fluttered past his face after the ball hit the floor. It would be perfect, he decided, for tying up Helen's beloved Winky Doll. He snatched it up.

As he struggled to make a knot – he'd never tied one before – his skin began to sting. It felt just like a nettle rash. He frowned. Then, to his amazement, the cloth began to melt and blend into the plastic surface of the doll. When the scrap had disappeared entirely, the toy began to glow bright blue.

Realising something was up, he shouted on his sister who, in turn, shouted on their mum.

"Mum! Joe's messing up my stuff!" She was looking forward to getting him into trouble.

She moved closer to see what he was up to but stopped dead in her tracks. Their mouths fell open at the same time.

Helen's beloved Winky Doll had come alive.

* * *

There Helen's doll stood, in the doorway of the cupboard, blinking and rubbing its eyes. The creature smiled up at Wee Joe and Helen, winking. It clapped its hands excitedly.

"Mummy!" Wee Joe and Helen screamed at the same time. They backed away from the cupboard, unsure what effect their shouting would have on the hairy, pixie-like creature. It still bore some resemblance to the Winky Doll, but was now taller and much uglier.

They watched, mouths gaping, as the little creature's neck and body momentarily pulsated like a boa constrictor's swallowing dinner. When it had stopped convulsing, the doll stretched its arms and legs as if waking from a long sleep.

More alert now, the strange creature jumped out of the cupboard and ran past them into the hall. It skidded past the hamster's cage and bounded up onto the windowsill, naked apart from a scrap of the Winky Doll's dress. It sat down with a thud.

Wee Joe pointed as he gave Helen a kick to get her attention. "Wook! Its head is awll flat and squished."

But Helen didn't want to look. She had already seen enough. She trembled. What was taking her mum so long?

"Wheere ees Mendel?" the creature asked in a high, husky, voice that faded into a wheeze.

Startled, Helen and Wee Joe took a step back. The creature was still changing shape.

"W...w...what?" Helen couldn't believe what she was seeing, and now hearing.

"You're bad!" Wee Joe pointed at the creature accusingly, impatiently brushing his overlong blond bangs out of his eyes with his other hand. "You're a gobwin."

"Hee hee hee... Not exactleee, leetle one," it replied.

The hamster wheel stopped spinning and there was a rustle amongst the shredded paper. Wee Joe saw the creature glance across at the cage.

"You better weeve Mufty awone!" Wee Joe warned, "or you'll get a smwack!"

The creature only sniggered.

* * *

Panting from their second sprint up the stairs in five minutes, Cathy and Jean threw open the bedroom door.

"Now what?" called Jean.

Helen and Wee Joe, however, were staring, transfixed, at the bedroom window.

Jean followed their gaze and gasped.

An ugly, blue-skinned creature was tapping its heels against the wall under the windowsill, busily picking its nose with a strangely elongated thumb.

"Argghhh!" screamed everyone. Everyone except Wee Joe, who calmly picked up the TV remote control.

The creature, about two feet tall, was a bit shorter

than Wee Joe. Full of determination, and lacking any fear, Wee Joe pulled the little blue doll-thing down off the windowsill by its left leg and smacked it full force in the face with the remote.

Now it was the creature's turn to scream. "Eeeeghh! Leetle bratee!" It cowered underneath the swinging curtains. "Whatcheee do dat feer? Eeeeghh!" It whimpered and scowled, baring its tiny needle teeth at Joe before fixing its sorrowful gaze on Jean. "Don't let leetle bratee hurt Eethan. Eethan wants to help ees!"

Jean looked at the blue creature with his strangely familiar pink loincloth. "What?"

"'What?'" Eethan mimicked Jean's surprised tone and giggled riotously.

"Mendel, ees used thee Creestal, haseent eee?" he continued.

"Who?" Cathy was swiftly regaining her composure. "What are you? Where did you come from? And who is Mendel?"

Eethan looked confused for a second then replied, "Blue Man, Denthan, and ee fish...at dee moment." He burst into another fit of giggles.

Wee Joe was about to give Eethan another smack with the remote, but Jean intercepted the weapon mid-swipe. "No, Joe! It's not nice to hit people...eh...things."

"I ees Blue Man. Not thing!" Eethan corrected. "Yee know Mendel, so you do. Yeees do." Eethan pointed an accusing, spindly finger at Cathy.

"The only Mendel I've ever heard of is that genetics bloke who studied peas," said Cathy, remembering something from her school days. Then she thought for a moment. "You don't mean that stinking fish James has in his room? He's in big trouble for that one. Thinks I don't know about it, but—"

"One en dee same!" Eethan clapped his hands and little

blue sparks pinged out from his fingertips. "One en dee same!" he repeated excitedly.

"What do you want with a goldfish?" she demanded.

Thoughtfully, Eethan clawed his chin with his long fingers.

When he didn't answer, Cathy snapped, "You can have the stinky thing!"

"Stinkee es nice. Mee likes stinkee!" Eethan slapped his thighs and vibrated with laughter again. He plumped down on a pile of boxed games.

Helen began to titter.

Jean threw her a cautionary look.

Cathy thought it was a good look and wondered why Jean didn't use it more often. A bit more discipline in the Harrison household wouldn't go amiss.

Wee Joe reached for the nearest hard toy, which happened to be a small, wooden sword. "Tell dat goblin not to sit on my stuff or I'll hit him again!"

"No!" Eethan and Jean shouted at the same time.

Cathy bent down to pick the creature up, but Eethan was too quick for her. Giggling, he ran between her legs and raced down the stairs, the others following.

"Bero!" Jean shouted. "Where's Bero?" Now that she thought about it, she hadn't seen the dog for almost an hour.

"Craig took him for a walk. Went to spray him with that flea stuff, or something," Helen recalled, her eyes still locked onto the blue creature as he bolted out the front door.

Jean watched with the others as Eethan hopped and skipped down her path. At the gate, he skidded to a halt and smiled back at them. Then, pointing up at the hill above Drumfintley, he squeaked, "You must follow meee! Jeesus Savees!" He gestured that they should follow, then shot off in the direction of the underpass.

They all stared after him in disbelief.

Wee Joe, however, was looking elsewhere. Cathy followed his gaze to see what was distracting him.

"Der's something not right. Something missing," said Wee Joe.

Cathy stared at the church tower and realised that Wee Joe was right, one of the gargoyles was missing.

It was almost half past seven.

17

A Slight Delay

It had grown extremely cold during the night and a thin layer of frost covered the boys' clothes. Fortunately, Bero had acted as a giant hot water bottle, keeping them warm enough to sleep through most of the night.

Now, however, the old dog had moved away and their teeth were beginning to chatter. There was a chill in their bones as a bitter morning breeze blew through the trees. Shivering, the boys opened their eyes to see little brown patches on the forest floor. Fingers of sunlight had found a way in through the branches to melt patterns on the frosty earth.

James sat up and stared in wonder as all kinds of insects, bigger than any they'd ever seen at home, fluttered round the giant tree trunks and burred between the branches. He felt a shiver trace his spine as he thought he spotted several of the moth creatures that had attacked them in the stone circle.

"*Flateria Zentalophus*," Mendel remarked, already darting past the little window of his barrel. He'd read James's thoughts. "Zental Moths. Harmless enough when they're not swarming."

Craig yawned. "Mendel, you know that James thinks you make up all those Latin names. Don't you, James?" Craig winked at his friend and rubbed his cold, bare legs as Bero waddled back over to them.

Mendel pushed an angry eye against the window. He focused on Craig. "They are not Latin names! The nomenclature predates Latin by over ten thousand years!"

Mendel sounded most miffed. "Where do you think Latin came from in the first place?"

"I don't know," shrugged Craig, not caring in the slightest.

"Zental Moths are only dangerous when they swarm round their queen," snapped Mendel. "They were sent to Drumfintley to scare us off. Dendralon knows that Sleven has failed him so now he will take other measures to delay us. Of course, he will kill us if he can. He too has read the prophecies that surround the talisman."

"He's in trouble," said James, putting two and two together.

"Unless he kills us soon," said Mendel.

"Brilliant," moaned Craig. "Cheery bloomin' cheery."

Finished with his lecture, Mendel splashed about more vigorously than usual before finally settling.

As the suns eased themselves above the eastern and western horizons, the frost on their clothes melted and they set off again, heading for the Eden Tree.

It was James who heard the distant rumbling first. Like far off thunder, the sound rolled, stopped, and then drummed once more. With each boom the noise grew louder, making Bero whimper. The old dog tucked his tail between his legs and flattened his droopy, mismatched ears.

"Mendel, what is that racket?" asked James.

Mendel stopped splashing and listened. "Osgrunfs, I shouldn't wonder."

"Os-whats?" asked Craig, grimacing as a sharp branch jagged his shin under the layer of fog.

"Giant, hairy, heavily-armed killing machines that show no mercy," explained Mendel.

The boys stared hard at each other for a long moment. "Brilliant," they said in unison.

"Osgrunfs don't usually come this far west," mused

Mendel. "We need to be ready." The wizard-goldfish mumbled to himself and James soon felt the knock, knock, knocking sensation that meant magic was a-brewing.

"Swwawwrdlive, Firewwtwwongueww!" James bubbled.

Craig was incredulous.

Then James said, "Spwwearwliwve, Gwwreewwn-wwormww!" The actual words – Swordlive, Firetongue, Spearlive, and Greenworm – were clear inside the boys' heads.

At first, a blue-tinged fog swirled round their feet in neat little circles, then it sparked and cracked like drips of water hitting hot oil.

Craig looked frightened as the fog rose over him and gathered round his right arm. "No more snakes, please!" he yelped, staring hard at James.

The same crackling fog shot up James's back then wisped down his right arm. It spun faster and faster around his hand. "Mendel!" cried James. "What's happening?"

Craig felt something heavy land in his hand, but screamed and let it fall, feeling as though he'd been scalded.

James had the same problem. "It's too hot!" he yelled.

Both boys were almost in tears with the pain.

"Quickly. Put your hands in the stream," Mendel directed.

Craig and James both crawled across to the flowing water and plunged their stinging hands straight in. To their relief, the pain immediately subsided. Feeling better, they withdrew their hands and peered down in amazement.

A picture of a green serpent had been burned – or perhaps tattooed – into the centre of Craig's palm. On James's palm there was a red bird-like creature with a lion's head, every feather and claw detailed.

"It looks incredible, but my mum will kill me!" blurted James. "She hates tattoos!"

"What a shocker," mocked Craig. "My dad's got one, a big anchor with 'My Jean' written below it."

"Yeah, but your dad probably wasn't eleven when he got his!" James retorted.

"Boys!" Mendel shouted. "We must focus!"

The trees were really shaking now, showering them with dead leaves and branches.

The fish-wizard's voice was tired, weakened by the magic he had just performed. "The Osgrunfs are getting closer," whispered Mendel. "Hold up your hand, James, and say 'Firetongue'." He directed Craig to do the same, but to say 'Greenworm' instead.

As James said the strange word, about three yards away the heavy object he'd dropped to the ground shot up from the mist and landed squarely in his hand, settling easily in his grip.

It was the most beautiful sword he'd ever seen. The graceful shape of the red bird-like creature was etched into the dull grey metal of the blade. A lion's head faced towards the sword's tip, its mouth open as though about to bite, while its mane swept back down the length of the blade.

The creature's tail feathers swirled onto, then over, the hilt. The handle, covered with soft red and gold leather, balanced perfectly in James's hand. It seemed to mould itself to his fingers. James knew the sword should be heavy – he'd heard the thud when it hit the ground – but it felt as light as a feather.

Behind him there was another low rumble followed by a resounding crash that made the whole forest shake uncontrollably for several minutes.

Finally the quake stopped and in the relative silence he heard Mendel shout, "Quick, Craig, say your word!"

"Oh...eh. What was it again?"

"Greenworm!" Mendel cried hoarsely, his patience waning.

"Greenworm!" hollered Craig, looking sheepish.

A stick-like object rose from the forest floor mist, flew over to Craig, and settled in his right hand. Lifting it high, Craig stared at the most amazing spear he'd ever seen. It was about four feet long with a metallic green hue. A dragon-like serpent was etched masterfully on the spearhead.

"I wanted a sword!" complained Craig, a petulant frown spreading over his freckled face.

"For goodness sake, Craig," Mendel exclaimed, "just get *down!*"

Bero, on hearing Mendel say 'down', dropped to the ground behind a fallen tree. Craig and James quickly followed suit.

Seconds later, the whole forest shook again. This time the deep, rumbling sound vibrated in their stomachs. James felt sick.

Peering out from their hiding place, the boys watched in horror as thousands of unusually tall creatures thundered past them like a stampede of wildebeest.

There was a blur of steel and hair for about twenty seconds, and then the strange beasts just stopped. Without warning, a stench, which vaguely resembled the odour of putrefying cheese, filled the forest. It caught at the backs of the boys' throats, making them want to gag. They quickly pinched their noses to shut out the rancid reek.

Why do so many creatures in this world smell so bad? James wondered.

Through the rootlets and ferns they could see the growling mass of evil standing only ten feet from them. The Osgrunfs looked like oversized sloths. Their bodies even had the same slouching posture and snub-nosed faces. Long, greenish-brown hair covered their bodies. It poked out, here and there, through openings in their strange armour.

James felt his palms go moist when he spied the long, hooked claws hanging down from the ends of the Osgrunfs' hairy limbs like grotesque, unkempt fingernails. Amazingly, these misshapen hands held all manner of weapons – swords, pikes, maces, even double-headed axes. They chinked and clanged together as the panting beasts attempted to regain their breath and prepare for the next charge.

Terrified, the boys pushed themselves flat against the forest floor.

Clouds of flies buzzed and pestered the Osgrunfs, causing them to snap at each other in frustration.

A shout cut through the din: "Harka!"

The harsh voice came from a giant of a creature. It stood a good head and shoulders above the others. Not only was his crimson armour shinier and in better condition, it was also more elaborate. An assortment of deadly spikes and hooks jutted from the elbows and knees.

James reckoned the beast's shield was the size of his kitchen table back home, and his spiked axe had to be at least twelve feet long. The huge throng made way for him, clanking and clattering as they scrambled to make room.

He was very close now and both boys noticed something familiar hanging round his hairy neck: a blue crystal, similar to the one they'd left in Drumfintley. It shimmered enticingly in the light filtering through the canopy above.

Walking through the ranks, the Osgrunf leader appeared to be inspecting his army's armour and weapons, poking at pikes not held high enough and badly skewed helmets. Finally, seemingly satisfied, the beast took a deep breath and called out once more, "Harka!"

Almost before the cry had left his mouth the whole herd began to move as one.

For quite some time, their thunderous charge shredded branches and tore through the undergrowth like a tornado as wave after wave passed the boys' position.

"Well, that was bloomin' scary!" breathed Craig when the last Osgrunfs had finally disappeared.

James stood up and stared at the red sword in his hand. Cautiously, he tapped it against the bark of the fallen tree they'd hidden behind. He stared, open-mouthed, as sparks of crimson whizzed up amongst the flying woodchips.

"Don't play with that!" snapped Mendel. "If you only knew what you were holding you would—"

"I would what?" challenged James, smarting at the reprimand.

"You would show a lot more *respect* for things..." Mendel's words trailed off again as the roar of the Osgrunf army faded into the forest. "They're heading straight for Gwendral," he muttered, half to himself. "Dendralon's obviously no fool."

"Hey, that big one had one of your crystals round his neck," Craig pointed out.

"His name is Hushna. He is the Osgrunfs' crystal barer." Mendel circled in the barrel for a moment. "Dendralon must have tricked them into attacking Gwendral," he continued after some thought. "The Hedra wizard must know how to operate the Magic Scales. This is not good."

James lifted his gaze from his sword and stared into the plastic window of the barrel. "Scales...? Do you think he's going to try to turn Gwendral into a giant portal using that crystal?"

"He can't without the talisman, right?" added Craig.

"He thinks he can," replied Mendel.

"How?" asked James.

"There is dark, Hedra necromancy afoot here," said Mendel. "I refuse to perform the evil required by the Hedra wizards."

James continued to examine his sword. "So he can turn the city into a gateway without the talisman?"

Mendel sighed deeply. "With enough Manimal sacrifice and the complete obliteration of the other races, it is possible."

James felt slightly mollified after having been snapped at by Mendel earlier.

Mendel's voice was unsteady, as if he'd just received bad news. "Right now he needs Hushna's crystal to operate the gateway. He needs to balance the Scales. But why," he pondered, "has the whole herd gone to the city in full battle armour? What has Dendralon promised the Osgrunfs to lure them there?"

James had neither any clue what Dendralon might have told the Osgrunfs, nor what relevance any scales had to the operation of the ark-like city of Gwendral, but he did know that he didn't want to see the Osgrunfs ever again, especially their leader, Hushna.

"We should wait for the smell and noise of the Osgrunfs to fade before moving off," said Mendel.

"Good plan," James muttered under his breath.

While they waited, Craig examined his spear. "Mendel, it probably hasn't crossed your mind, but I'm not too comfortable holding this thing." He tapped the spear against a moss-covered stone. "I mean, I don't really know how to use it, and I'm not sure that I want to either."

"What do you mean?" James yelped, swinging his sword like a knight of old. "These weapons are great!"

"Firstly," Mendel cut in, "let me explain where we are. The Forest of Eldane is one of the most dangerous places you could possibly imagine. For over thirteen thousand years this forest has stood between the cliffs of Nordengate, behind us, and the steppes of Gwendral ahead. As the first saplings pushed their way up through the cold soil, long dormant creatures began to stir and venture above ground, the Osgrunfs being one of the first to appear. They were one of the few races able to adapt to the bright light. Extremely powerful, they are hated and feared by all, even the Hedra. You will need some kind of protection against them, for we are sure to encounter them again. Secondly, don't worry about using your weapons, they will do the work for you. If you hurt or kill anything, it will be the work of the magical weapons, not you."

"Oh, and that makes it alright, does it?" said Craig. "Kill, guilt free, or your money back, is that it?"

"Look, you stupid boy," Mendel's voice sounded sharp, "if a Hedra were to pop out of the forest now and attempt to chew your head off, are you telling me you would refuse to defend yourself, on moral grounds?"

"So where do the Hedra come from?" asked James, anxious to dampen Mendel's anger. He glanced nervously round the undergrowth before lifting up his rucksack. It was time to get moving. Besides, Mendel was starting to sound aggressive, too much like his mum, and that was never good.

"The Hedra, as I've already explained, are reptilian creatures. They've lived in the southern marshes for many years now. Their correct name is *Hedritica nubula—*"

"Do we really need to know the Latin names for every bloomin' thing?" Craig hated what he thought of as useless details. "I mean, it's all very interesting and stuff," he went on, his bored expression belying his words, "but I'll never remember any of it, so what's the point?"

"*Nubulatis!*" Mendel finished stubbornly, ignoring Craig's plea. Splashing his tail, he issued a disparaging, "Harumph!" followed by, "And I told you, it's not Latin," and fell silent.

"I think he's in a huff," whispered Craig to James.

"Yeah, nice one, numpty," James whispered back.

* * *

In silence, the two boys and the dog trudged onward. They followed a faint pathway that headed southeast, towards the small sun Mendel had called Zalion. It was hopefully also the same direction as the island of Senegral and the Eden Tree.

After about a mile of scrambling over fallen trees and jagged vines, James turned to Craig. "I can't believe how great this feels. Back home I could never have made this hike without using my stupid inhaler every five minutes."

"I suppose I take breathing for granted," Craig replied, suddenly stopping and kneeling down. Something had caught his attention. "What's this?"

James quickly joined his friend. There, amidst the leaves and brush, was a shiny piece of metal. Caught in a slender ray of sunlight, it glinted and winked invitingly.

"Is that what I think it is?" asked Craig.

James felt his pulse quicken. "Yes. Yes it is!" James tentatively touched the metal, then pulled it free of the dead leaves. It was a little silver-coloured compass, hinged in the middle, with a sharp pin on one end and a pencil holder on the other.

"It's Dad's," whispered James, his eyes welling with tears.

"It does seem a bit out of place here," Craig acknowledged. "But you can't be *entirely* sure it's your dad's, can you?" He sounded almost smug about it.

"I am *absolutely* sure it's his," James snapped, "because *I* bought it for him." He searched out Bero. "Mendel!" James lifted the barrel until its plastic window was just a few inches from the metal compass. "It's Dad's – the one he always uses when he's orienteering. It took me ages to find him a compass with a brass hinge like this. I've seen him use it tons of times. That proves it, he's here."

James stood and scanned the forest. "Dad!" His small voice could barely be heard above the general din of screeches and howls that surrounded them.

Mendel floated over to the window of the barrel to take a look. "We don't use such instruments in Denthan, so..." He tilted slightly to stare up at James.

"So?" repeated James.

"So, one logical explanation may be that your father is here after all," admitted Mendel.

"I knew it!" James smiled as he sucked on his thumb, having pricked it with the needle-sharp pin. "I was right!"

"But," interrupted Mendel, "there is also the distinct possibility that Dendralon is leading us into a trap."

"What are you on about?" hissed James, his mind summersaulting with good and bad thoughts.

"Dendralon is very aware of the prophecies surrounding the talisman. He may, in fact, have planted that compass to lead us astray."

A heartbeat later, James realised this meant his dad might not be around after all.

18

The Centides

In silence, the boys picked their way through the undergrowth, often passing through golden shafts of light that crisscrossed the forest floor. The occasional giant bug fluttered round their heads before flying off, while unknown creatures continuously slithered out of their way. Large moss-covered roots rising up out of the earth meant they had to scramble and climb more often than not to make any headway.

After an hour of hard going, Craig noticed that Bero's back legs were beginning to play up.

"What happened to the path?" he asked. He knew that Bero couldn't keep up the pace much longer.

James shrugged and Mendel did not reply either. Not even one moody splash or grumpy blub.

"What's wrong with you, Mendel?" James asked. He kept thinking about becoming separated from the wizard goldfish in this place, and how terrifying it would be. At the same time, he was desperately trying to imagine what the talisman might look like. If he could find it quickly, things might be a lot easier. He traced his fingers over jutting stones and reached up to touch odd-looking seeds or branches as they moved.

"You're not still in a huff, are you?" added Craig. He knelt down and tapped on the barrel.

James slid to a halt beside Craig. "He doesn't like that. You know he doesn't."

"Do you think he knows where we are?" said Craig, staring around the dark forest.

"Of course he does," answered James. "He's probably just sleeping...or thinking. You know how he gets." James pointed to a brighter part of the forest up ahead. It seemed to be a little less dense.

"There's an opening across there. What do you think, Mendel? Should we head that way?" James bent and stared into the barrel, but there was no reply. Instead, his question was met by a drool-laden lick from Bero. "Yuk! Craig, your dog's breath really stinks."

"Yeah, it's great, isn't it?" Craig laughed. "You know, if I was your dad, I would have gone that way too." Craig pointed to the clearing James had spotted. "We've got your sword and this." He gave his spear a violent shake.

"Hey, watch what you're doing with that thing!" exclaimed James, his gaze still fixed on the bright patch ahead. He sighed. "You might be right. Let's give it a try."

* * *

For about a mile, the going was much easier. But it wasn't long before the trees grew thicker again and the forest even darker than before. They also began to notice large, sticky patches on the forest floor.

Craig prodded the clear goo with his green spear. "Yuk. What is that stuff?"

James shrugged.

They continued walking, though more cautiously now. With every step, the number of blobs grew, forcing the boys to zigzag to avoid them. It was only when James happened to look up that he saw the probable cause of the mess.

Suspended above their heads, hundreds of glossy, black pods hung from the canopy like giant cocoons, reflecting the colours and shapes of the forest around them, making them virtually invisible. Swaying slowly in the breeze, the pods were held fast to the highest branches by long, gelatinous strands.

James bent down and peered into the barrel. In a sharp whisper he said, "Mendel! Wake up!" He tapped on the hard plastic.

"What...? Be careful!" Mendel's voice sounded both angry and groggy at the same time. "Never disturb a goldfish like that unless you want to kill it." He swam up to the plastic window. "Why did you leave the path, James? Why?"

James looked up at the pods. "We tried to ask you, but we thought you must have been tired or..."

"It was my idea," Craig intervened, coming to James's rescue.

James gave his friend a grateful look.

"I might have known," Mendel muttered. "Let me get my bearings." The wizard sloshed about noisily before pushing the familiar orange and black eye up against the plastic window of the barrel. "You dim-witted oafs!" Even though Mendel could see through James's eyes, he seemed to prefer the use of his own in a crisis. "Those are *Scolopendra*. But unfortunately for us, they are of the Denthan variation."

"*Scolowhatta*?" attempted Craig, his freckled nose wrinkled in confusion. "Sorry, mate, none the wiser!"

"They're Centides," Mendel explained.

"Oh, I see," said James.

Craig squinted at James. "You haven't got a blinking clue what he's on about, so don't start." He raised his spear and pointed at one of the pods. However, the weapon shimmered, made a little "puhh" noise, then vanished.

"My spear!" he shrieked.

"Oh no, not now..." James looked down at his sword, only to see it do the same thing.

Together he and Craig kicked about in the leaves, searching frantically for their lost weapons.

"You can stop doing that," Mendel scolded. "Your weapons are still close by. All you have to do is say your magic words and they'll be back in your hands ready for action."

"Whaow!" Craig smiled and clapped his hands.

Mendel flicked his tail. "Shhh! Keep as quiet as you can. We do not want to disturb them."

The boys could see that nearly every tree had at least five or six smooth pods hanging heavily from its branches. James moved closer to the nearest black shape. Its surface was like polished marble and his reflection, bent and distorted, resembled something from the Hall of Mirrors at the Easter fair. The pod twitched and he thought about the talisman again. *The talisman moves through ancient leaves and yet, at times, stands still. No Denthan eyes can see it; some say they never will.*

The pod twitched again.

"James, did you see that?" Craig whispered sharply.

James, his face still only inches away from the pod, appeared not to have heard.

"James!" yelled Mendel.

"Ughhh!" James gasped as a jet of black powder shot out of the pod, directly into his wide eyes and gaping mouth. A second later, a vicious pair of orange pincers, attached to long tentacles, burst free of the casing and whizzed past his ears. Without warning, the stalk that ended in the two pincers hit him in the chest, pushing him to the ground. The pincers snaked back over his face and began to close around his throat. They burrowed deep into the soil on either side of his neck, trapping him.

"Ughh! Help! Kuu! Kuuh!" he spluttered, choking from the black dust. Not only was he pinned to the ground, he was blind and struggling to breathe.

Bero, the only one not stunned into immobility by the surprise attack, barked loudly, then bounded forward. He sank his teeth into James's sleeve and pulled with all his might. Struggling, the dog shook his furry head and dug his paws deep into the leaf litter. He had managed to move James a couple of inches when a second, much bigger set of black-tipped pincers whipped from the top of the pod and thudded deep into the ground at the precise spot where James's legs had been.

Bero turned his attention to the tentacle holding James by the throat. His sharp teeth made quick work of the thinner appendage.

James sat up, his eyes stinging like mad. He was wheezing terribly and felt completely disoriented, but knew it was now up to him to get away from the pod. Using his feet and elbows, he backpedalled, while Bero continued to pull on his sleeve. Together, they succeeded in moving another few feet.

The pod tore open from top to bottom, spilling its wet, orange cargo squirming and squealing onto the ground. James could feel warm black liquid seeping over his feet and legs as he slipped and struggled a few more inches away.

"Craig!" Mendel shouted. "Say your command word. Say it!"

"I...I...can't remember it. You s...s...You say it!" Craig stuttered.

"Craig!" screamed James.

"*You* have to say it!" Mendel screeched.

"Greentongue," he tried. "No...no...Um, Greenbums? Argh! Not even close! Greenworm?"

The spear appeared in Craig's hand just as the fully emerged Centide rose up on several sets of legs. The deadly bug attempted to pull its pincers free of the soil, the segmented antennae on its terrifyingly large insect head flicking and writhing with the effort.

Triumphant, the giant insect clicked its black-tipped

mandibles and advanced.

James had scampered back a good ten feet by now, but had unwittingly stopped directly beneath another swinging pod.

Craig ran forward, swinging his spear in a perfect arc before him. The razor-sharp tip slashed between two orange and black segments, cutting the first giant centipede in two.

An eerie cry echoed throughout the forest as the Centide's two halves thrashed about, spilling even more black, steaming liquid over the forest floor.

Craig saw that the second Centide had begun to cut through its pod. Within seconds its many legs were free and it was preparing to drop onto James's head.

Without any conscious command on his part, the green spear shot from Craig's hand and plunged itself deep into the black sack.

Inside, the creature convulsed, jerked twice, and fell still.

Mendel's frantic voice filled their heads. "Run! Now!"

Craig pulled James to his feet and dragged him along. Hundreds of the twitching pods heaved and writhed over their heads. It felt as if they were running through a horrendous children's adventure park; only the obstacles were not squidgy foam-rubber animals but stiff, shiny pods holding the deadliest of contents.

"You've triggered an emergence!" announced Mendel excitedly. "Each pod...has a receptor that reacts to...carbon-dioxide and temperature change, and your breathing has generated both. They're releasing pheromones. They're actually talking to each other!"

The boys couldn't believe that in the middle of complete chaos the little fish was trying to give them a biology lesson.

"You gormless guppy!" Craig screeched. "There's

nothing wonderful about it!" He was hauling James along while his spear sliced and stabbed at the reaching creatures. "Do something, you useless old fart!"

The black dust from the hatching pods was blinding and choking Craig now too.

Sharp, poisonous mouthparts reached out, searching for flesh. James could hear them clacking and hissing as, behind them, hundreds of legs fumbled onto the forest floor for the first time.

"Craig, I can't see. Get us out if here!"

Craig began to panic. "I can't see either! I can't s—"

The ground beneath them suddenly dropped away.

Bero barked as they all tumbled over the edge of a ravine. Landing heavily on their backs, they slid on the moss and mud, picking up speed as they fell. Faster and faster, they tore down the slope until they flew off the edge of the gorge.

* * *

They seemed to be in mid-air for minutes, but it must have been seconds. Just when they thought they must be done for, they splashed into something cold, wet and fast-moving. It was a river, and unfortunately for them, it was in full flow.

Caught in the roaring torrent, they were swept downstream like Pooh sticks. Half submerged, the boys and Bero tried to push themselves away from the jagged rocks, cutting their hands on the sharp edges.

James gasped for air every time his head broke the surface.

At least the cold water had washed the black, stinging powder from their eyes. They could see again, but choked as they struggled and kicked to keep their heads above the heaving surface.

Eventually they were thrown onto a small, shale beach.

Soaked through and numb with cold, they huddled against each other for warmth as they cast their eyes over the steep slopes of the ravine. Thankfully, there was no sign of the Centides.

Bero shook himself, giving the boys one last dousing. Less weighed down by water now, his tail began the familiar, silly wag they knew so well.

James pulled himself further up the shale beach then rolled onto his back. "Craig, are you okay?"

Without looking at James, Craig nodded and gave him a thumbs-up. "Soaked, but I'll dry." He flashed a familiar toothy grin as he reached for Bero.

James watched as Craig teased Bero's fur. Something was wrong. He studied Bero for a moment longer before realising what it was.

"Mendel?" James threw himself towards the big Golden Retriever and felt for his collar. "Where's the brandy barrel?"

Craig's grin evaporated. The barrel was gone.

They ran up and down the riverbank shouting for Mendel, keeping it up until they were exhausted and completely hoarse.

But there was no reply.

James was shaking. "Now what?" He was scared. His throat ached and his eyes still stung. He closed his eyes in bitter contemplation. "He *knew* he was going to leave us. He planned this whole thing! He kept going on about getting separated from us, and now I have no chance of finding the talisman. Not without him."

"Yes you have," scolded Craig. "He said you would know what it was."

"Not without his magic."

"Rubbish," snapped Craig. "And he didn't know that he would be smashed against the rocks in that river." Craig flicked his fingers in the direction of the fast-flowing water.

"It's weird to hear you, of all people, defending him like that," said James in a much quieter voice.

Craig shrugged his shoulders and cuddled into Bero's wet fur. "I shouldn't have called him an 'old fart'," he muttered.

"No," agreed James.

Tealfirth, the larger of the two suns, had dimmed and reddened.

Craig flopped back onto the shale beach and Bero licked his face. "We're in big trouble now, old pal," he told the dog. "Big trouble..." He turned to James. "But you and me are going to find that talisman before it's too late."

19

The Gathering

Dendralon closed his eyes and formed a picture in his mind of the Gorton Sea. The immense body of water stretched out towards the western horizon like an endless mirror, merging seamlessly with a cloudless sky. A few small ripples lapped against the dark brown beaches that stretched endlessly north and south. Only a spattering of islands marred the horizon.

Below the tranquil surface, however, something moved. In a series of straight lines that stretched over twenty miles back into the depths, the water bubbled and boiled, the disturbance growing more intense as it neared the shore. Far beneath, long lines of Salteth, the warrior slaves of the Salt Trolls, followed their underwater masters' pathways to the shore. Rising to the surface, they snapped and gargled. Soon they would have to depend on their rudimentary lungs to survive.

The Salteth were barely three feet high, with crested heads, tiny holes for ears and smooth, green skin. In their webbed hands they carried kelp nets and hooks made from sharpened coral. On the shore, they wove in and out amongst the twenty-foot-tall Salt Trolls. In the bright morning light, the leathery-skinned giants blinked their great orb-like eyes. Flaking crusts of salt dropped off their hulking grey flesh as they walked. They supported themselves on long jagged spears made from the saw teeth of Gnarwhales. The stench of rotting fish that preceded the horde wafted high over the city walls of Gwendral like a terrifying warning.

The mass of bodies clambered up the wet sand and scrambled over the rocks, heading straight for the City of Spires. The bigger Trolls often flicked the puny Salteth out of the way, or simply crushed them under foot.

High-pitched whines echoed over the beaches as the trampled Salteth squirmed in pain, a live snack for the Salt Trolls, but more often eaten by their own kind in a few awful moments of frenzied feasting.

Swarms of flies had gathered and now hung in a permanent cloud above the misshapen sea creatures.

Dendralon opened his eyes and smiled to himself. As he had foreseen, the city of Gwendral was in panic. The evacuation was gathering momentum.

Some fifteen thousand fierce Osgrunfs had already taken over the fields surrounding the city walls. The mass sacrifice required to perform his ancient Hedra magic was only hours away.

The dark wizard closed his eyes again, anxious to see more. Centides, recently released from their pods, had gathered round the edges of the Osgrunfs' camp, while several lumbering Tree Trolls congregated at the edge of the forest, wary enough to keep their distance from the clawed Osgrunfs in their spiked armour.

The reptilian Hedra had pushed on and now covered the entire ridge south of the main gates, impatiently awaiting their chance to retake the city that had once been theirs. For generations, their need for revenge had never faltered. Nor had their hatred of the Manimals. Now, Dendralon looked west towards the sea, to where more than twenty thousand Salteth and their lumbering Salt Troll masters hissed at the skies and shook their bleached spears in defiance.

All was going to plan...

* * *

Back in Drumfintley, all was about to change...

Jean turned to Cathy. "That thing wants us to follow him."

"Yes, but should we take the kids?" Cathy hoped Jean would say no.

"We have to. I can't leave them here alone!" argued Jean, lifting Bero's lead from the hook in the shoe cupboard and stuffing it in her pocket.

"Well, c'mon, let's get after him," Cathy grumbled.

"What about James and Craig?" asked Helen, her eyes still wide with excitement.

"He's got dem!" Wee Joe's comment made them all stop for a second.

"I don't see how," remarked Jean.

"Oh, that's just great," said Cathy. "I'll run ahead and check at my house on the way."

They hurried out through Jean's front door and up the path after the little blue man.

* * *

Loosening his dog collar, Father Michael took one last look down Willow Terrace before turning the corner that led to the underpass. The dark corrugated tunnel had been built at the same time as the dual carriageway and was about twenty yards long. It led to the farm track that wound up the hillside, through Tank Woods, and eventually onto Bruce Moor. The bypass overhead was extremely dangerous, always busy with tourist traffic heading north. Judging by the excessive noise above him, today was no exception.

Michael made his way up the tunnel, picking up Patch to ensure the little Jack Russell didn't cut her paws on the broken glass that littered the dank floor of the underpass. He was almost through, when he stopped in his tracks.

There was something up ahead. Frightened, he sucked in a lungful of stale air and rubbed his eyes. He was positive he'd seen a shape jump across the light that marked the end of the tunnel.

"I must be imagining things," he whispered to himself, struggling to keep hold of Patch. The dog had become wriggly all of a sudden.

With a bark, she leapt out of his arms and flew up the remainder of the tunnel, yapping and growling until she disappeared into the bright light at the end. Then, two or three seconds later, Michael heard a sharp hiss, and saw Patch dashing back towards him. She ran as fast as her little legs could take her, squealing and yelping the entire way.

"Patch?" He tried to catch sight of her in the darkness, but the little dog found him first, jumping straight back up into his arms.

"What was it, girl?" Patch whined as she snuggled beneath Michael's black jacket.

Cautiously, Michael moved forward, towards the end of the tunnel. Patch's little heart pounded furiously against his chest. He almost turned to go back towards the safety of Drumfintley, but then regained some courage and walked forward again. He couldn't let the local yobs get the better of him.

He had just reached the opening at the end of the tunnel when a small voice shouted "Boo!" behind him.

"Arghh!" Michael cried out, squinting over his shoulder as he crouched.

"Yip! Yip! Yip!" Patch barked and growled, staring up at the tunnel's roof.

"What's going on?" Michael shouted, spinning round. "Where are you?" He steadied himself against the cold, ridged wall of the tunnel. "I don't think your prank is funny in the least!" he scolded, trying to sound brave.

"Up heeere!" the voice whispered.

He jerked his head back and looked up at the corrugated ceiling. To his amazement, a tiny blue man, wearing nothing except a pink piece of cloth, was clinging to the roof above him. The material fluttered in the summer breeze.

"Neeece to meeet you, Fatheeer!"

Michael gulped.

Above Michael and Patch's heads, the little blue man darted this way and that, sticking to the corrugated ceiling like a spider.

"Have eee seeen Mendel?" Eethan directed the question at Michael but immediately answered it himself. "No, ee don't sense eet! No."

"Have you...?" the little blue man started, but then screeched, "Eee!"

* * *

Meanwhile, Ephie Blake was panting and puffing up the slope towards the same corrugated underpass. She'd seen Father Michael disappear into the tunnel and wanted to catch up before he got too far.

As she sorted her hair, she heard his little dog barking madly. The racket was amplified and distorted into a non-stop clatter that made her head thump.

She heard Michael cry out above the din. Was the Peck boy setting about him again?

"Oh, dear, what's happening?" Ephie whispered to herself. Then she called out, "Father Michael?"

"Ephie Blake!" a harsh voice replied.

Ephie almost jumped out of her skin.

* * *

Cathy Peck had thrown on the first thing she had laid her hands on – one of her missing husband's fleecy jackets – and reached the underpass before Jean and the kids.

"Who are you spying on this time, Ephie?"

Ephie spun, her momentum almost taking her over.

"Spying, spying? I'm not spying on anybody!"

Cathy watched her stuff a hand into the pocket of her coat.

"How many bars of tablet have you gone through so far tonight? Two? Three?"

Cathy heard Jean Harrison and her youngsters approaching and curbed her interrogation.

They were all clustered round the entrance to the underpass when a small dog ran out, straight towards them.

"It's Patch!" cried Helen.

One second later, Cathy and Jean were back in the comfort of Jean's living room. They had just put down their coffee and bitten into their second tea cake.

The time loop set by Mendel had run its course. It was once again 19:15:01 on Sunday, the twenty-second of June.

* * *

Immune to the time loop's repetition, Eethan dropped to the tunnel floor and muttered to himself. Then he tittered, and clapped his hands. "Ah, yes! Loop dee loop...loop dee loop!" His voice echoed down the metal tunnel, eventually fading into the noise of the traffic outside.

Eethan knew how to stop the time loop. Unless he did so the others would not be able to follow him, and he needed them all. Even the nasty little bratty one. So with a long sigh, which ended in a churlish snigger, he bolted up the forestry track and through Tank Woods as fast as a startled hare. Out into the orange twilight of

Bruce Moor he sprang, leaping high above the heather as he scampered towards the Jesus Rocks.

As he ran, his shape changed again. He now bore little resemblance to the toy that had given him life. His blue skin shone in the twilight as his fine, downy hair began to slough off then blow away like dandelion seeds. A tell-tale trail of white fanned out behind him.

Stepping inside the Jesus Rocks, he continued to chuckle and mutter to himself as he made his way towards the biggest stone.

For several seconds, he sniffed about until he found the blue crystal, still pointing towards Ben Larvach. Eethan picked up the shining gem, placed it on the palm of his hand and waited.

After a few seconds, the crystal began to melt into his skin like snow until, finally...with a hiss, it was gone.

"Uhhh...!" he groaned. This part always stung, but it also made him dizzy with exhilaration.

He thought back to when Mendel had found him on Hushwish Beach, far to the west, on the Isle of Harris. Outcast and alone, Eethan had been attacked by his own kind for refusing to drown some sailors struggling near the rocks.

From the start, Mendel had seemed fascinated by how magic flowed so easily from him. A mutual respect had blossomed and their ensuing adventures had made them the best of friends.

While his thoughts drifted peacefully back over the years, Eethan's body shook and changed once again. His skin became taut over his muscles, and his bones creaked and groaned as they lengthened. Within seconds, he had returned to his full height: three feet and two inches.

Feeling much better now, Eethan glanced into a peaty puddle to check on his reflection. His face had returned to its typical light grey. A shock of snowy white hair had replaced the doll's curly locks and now drooped lazily over his left eye. His body, though still blue, glittered red and gold in the evening sun.

"Eeeestephie nan ta chee la!" His hand placed on the Jesus Rock, Eethan shut his black eyes and whispered the phrase twice more.

A huge crack of thunder signalled the end of the time loop. A sudden gust of wind rattled through the heather and bushes as it swept down the hillside. Like an old steam train, time pushed forward, eventually getting itself back on track.

In Drumfintley, the seconds ticked forward once again.

The heron flapped past the church spire for the fourth time, but on this occasion, instead of starting over again, it sailed off into the cobalt sky above Loch Echty. A relieved cry rasped from its throat and it ruffled its feathers as though somehow understanding it was finally free from further delay.

Eethan knew that people from the village would, once again, be at the mouth of the underpass. Fate required everyone to attend, and he chuckled as he waited for them all to arrive at the Jesus Rocks.

* * *

In Denthan, everything was also racing towards a rendezvous with fate. Using the semicircle of stone scales in the Council Chamber, Dendralon had created a vision pool with which to watch the events unfolding outside the city. The Osgrunfs were growing restless, but Hushna, their giant leader, was keeping them in check under his 'Harka' command.

Swarms of flies darkened the skies above the stinking beasts as they squatted in the great Plain of Gwendral. Always on edge and eager to charge, they crouched in

Paul Murdoch

their dirty, battered armour and bickered. Their supplies were dwindling and the sight of Gwendral was goading them, generating a mixture of frustration and excitement.

This high speed, nomadic, berserker army viewed the other gathering hordes with complete disdain and a ravenous hunger. Fifteen-thousand-strong, the powerful Osgrunfs were capable of turning upon those they considered lesser beasts. Like a battering ram they could easily push through any resistance they might offer. If their wait was too long and their patience tested too far, perhaps they would. After all, they were undefeated in over one hundred years.

Using the dark Hedra magic of dream-delving, Dendralon had called Hushna to arms. Speaking to him in his sleep, Dendralon had told the Osgrunf leader that the gates of Gwendral would open wide for his race, and that all the powers and treasures within would be theirs if they helped the Hedra retake the city. He had told Hushna that there would be a great gathering of the races and to wait for his signal before acting. And he had told him that he would help them crush all others and reward them alone after the battle. Having travelled far and long, the Osgrunfs were ready – ready for battle and ready to reap those rewards.

Dendralon grinned as he watched Hushna toy with the blue crystal that hung round his neck.

Satisfied with what he saw, Dendralon turned his attention to the massive Salt Trolls. They had reached the city walls, their loose skin dropping to the soil in huge lumps as they walked. Now it was being swiftly replaced by the hardened scales needed to protect them from Denthan's twin suns. Huge shark skins, draped over their broad backs and shoulders, were both a kind of armour and an occasional food source. More typically, however, whenever the mood took them they just picked up the nearest Salteth and swallowed the tiny creature whole.

Sintor, King of the Salt Trolls, had dreamt the same dream as Hushna. In it, Athelstone had peeled the Manimal skin from his reptilian face and revealed himself as Dendralon, the ancient Hedra necromancer. He had then told Sintor that the Sea Trolls would be the sole recipients of his gratitude. "After the Manimals have run off in fear of the great gathering," he'd explained, "my Hedra and your army will obliterate all others. You will collect your share of the prize and forever be surrounded by mountains of gold."

Sintor possessed a blue crystal like Hushna's, but his was set in a thick bronze amulet that dug into the scaly flesh of his wrist. Dendralon saw him look up at Tealfirth. He knew that the heat would intensify and that the Troll King would not be able to keep his army at bay much longer.

The Salt Trolls' slaves, the Salteth, were forever pouring seawater over themselves to preserve their fragile skin, which had never truly evolved a remedy for the burning heat. Ceaselessly, they snapped and hissed at each other, their foul mood having much to do with their discomfort and hunger. The situation was so bad that the putrid parasites actually fought each other over the right to eat the Trolls' sloughed-off skin.

Dendralon knew that, like the Osgrunfs, both the Salteths and Trolls had no regard for the other races of Denthan; they would grow restless if the gates did not open soon. Their tempers were already close to breaking point.

Dendralon's own race, the Hedra, was a different case altogether. The Hedra King, Feldon, had organized the reptilian creatures into alternating rows of infantry and archers, extending all the way back to the edge of the marshes. To the southeast and southwest of the gates were numerous spearmen and chariots to guard the army's flanks. Lookouts had been posted and were constantly scanning for any signs of trouble from the Salt Trolls or Osgrunfs.

Before he'd donned King Athelstone's Manimal skin, Dendralon had paid a personal visit to Feldon and hammered home to him the importance of victory.

Besides Dendralon, Feldon was the only one who knew the truth about Tealfirth – that Denthan's largest sun was dying. He, too, recognised its flares for what they were – the death throes of an ancient star.

Because the Hedra had felt Tealfirth's heat longer than any other race on the planet, it had been easy for Dendralon to convince Feldon to follow his plan.

"There is space for only so many inside the city," he'd explained, "and since we were the first to evolve, we should be the last to survive. Our ancestors built Gwendral, therefore it is only right that we and our kind should be the ones to escape and rule other worlds. With my power and the original Hedra magic, we will forge a new beginning."

Soon Dendralon would be able to shed his degrading – and increasingly disgusting – disguise. Within a day or so, the Manimals would empty into the underground tunnels like the vermin they were, and the Hedra would take over the city. He did, however, wonder if he could recreate the Hedra magic needed to activate the gateway – to turn the whole city into a gigantic ark that would save them from the dying Denthan star.

The crystals needed to operate the Scales of Gwendral were within his grasp and the ten thousand souls needed for the final spell were gathered now – more, indeed. But still he worried that the meddlesome Mendel would find a way to return. Dendralon knew about the Manimal prophecies. They stated that the talisman could override the Hedra magic, shatter the great Scales of Gwendral and return power to the Manimals. He had to cover all the angles. He could not afford Mendel any chance of success.

20

The Second Going

As Patch bolted for the Drumfintley exit, Father Michael almost slipped in his efforts to follow the little pup. Breathing heavily, he felt his way along the metal sides of the underpass.

To his surprise, a crowd was gathered at the entrance, with people staring at him suspiciously.

Cathy Peck immediately began to interrogate him. "What's going on? Are you alright? Is Patch okay? Have you seen James and Craig?"

She's like a headmistress on adrenaline, thought Michael, still reeling from his encounter with what he could only describe as a little blue man. The thing had scuttled about on the roof of the underpass like a spider.

"Well," he began, "I'm not sure, really..." He noticed that his hands were shaking.

At that moment a violent rush of air roared out of the tunnel behind him, ruffling what little hair he had and spraying everyone with sand. They winced and shielded their eyes as the freak gale blew hard for several moments.

Everyone turned to Michael as the wind subsided. He was struggling to find the necessary words to describe what he'd just seen, but Wee Joe did it for him. The little boy looked up at him and asked, "Did the wee blue dolly man bite Patch?"

"It bites?" gasped Michael.

Ephie Blake stamped her foot. "What's going on here? I demand to know the truth!"

Patch interpreted the large woman's gesture as a threat

and sank her sharp teeth into Ephie's powder-blue joggers, jerking and bucking as Ephie tried to kick her off. The dog seemed intent on removing them altogether, but Michael grabbed the pup just in time and freed the joggers from her little teeth.

"Unhand me, you fiend!" Ephie shouted at the vicar, struggling desperately to heave her sportswear back into place.

"I was only trying to help," protested Michael, blushing.

"As sure as fudge you were!" Ephie threw the remains of her tablet at the vicar and gave a 'ha' of delight when a piece smacked off his bald head.

"Awch! Why...is everyone giving me such a hard time today?" yelped Michael.

"Oh shut up." Cathy had dismissed Michael with a flick of her fingers. "And as for you, Ephie, nobody's interested in removing your joggers, I can assure you. So either help us follow that...thing and find the boys, or bog off!"

"What thing?" said Ephie, bemused. "And there's no need to be so rude all the time, you..."

"Now, now!" Michael laughed nervously and picked up the little terrier.

Jean quickly explained that Craig, James and Bero were missing. "We think Eethan has something to do with it."

"Eethan? Who's Eethan?" Ephie demanded to know.

"He's a little blue man!" Cathy answered angrily. "So are you going to help look for the boys or not?" She threw Ephie a nasty smile.

Ephie frowned and returned Cathy Peck's challenge with a hateful stare and irritated sniff. She nonchalantly tried to flick her permed hair back to show she wasn't bothered. In the end, however, she heaved her joggers up even higher and moaned, "I'll come. Of course, I'll come." She dipped into the pockets of her Barbour jacket for more sweets, only to look up and see that the rest of the group had already moved on. "Wait!"

Cathy assigned Michael the task of baby-balancing; while Ephie, once she'd caught up, held Helen's hand, more for her own balance than out of any sense of duty.

In front, Cathy and Jean led the way towards Tank Woods.

"Are you sure the boys are up there?" Michael asked, steadying himself on a stone dyke as he adjusted Wee Joe on his hip.

Cathy Peck turned to face the reverend. "We're not *sure* where *anyone* is. We're just looking, okay?"

Jean cleared her throat "Eh...what Cathy means, is that we think Eethan..."

"De Gobwin," Wee Joe interpreted, helpfully.

Jean pressed on. "We believe he said something about the Jesus Rocks."

"Well, he certainly sounds like a good chap," mused Michael. He nodded his approval and caught Cathy's arm just as she slipped on a moss-covered stone.

Behind him, Ephie muttered, "As sure as fudge," several times in succession.

"Ave you got any den?" enquired Wee Joe, now perched high on Michael's shoulders. He could see much more from up there.

Ephie wasn't too comfortable around children. "Pardon, dear?"

"Fudge!" Wee Joe lowered his hand in anticipation.

"Emm, no, no I don't." Ephie slipped her hand in her pocket and fingered the several bars of tablet as if they were solid gold. Fudge...tablet...they were completely different things. She hadn't lied.

The path evened off a bit, making the going a little easier. Here and there they saw a muddy paw print and what looked like marks made by two sets of trainers. It was hard to be sure though, as the woodland floor appeared to be littered with dead moths in addition to the usual pine needles.

* * *

On a mission to freshen up the paint on the Jesus rocks, Archie MacNulty had just emerged from Tank Woods when he stopped in his tracks. He took a sharp intake of breath. "What the...?"

His gaze had settled on a little blue man standing boldly in front of the Jesus Rocks.

The creature pointed straight at Archie and smiled.

MacNulty didn't want to breathe, let alone admit to himself that the creature was anything more than a hallucination. Nonetheless, he stepped forward, his hand gripping his paintbrush. He checked his poacher's pocket and, sure enough, his favourite ferret, Sarge, was curled up inside. It gave him a strange sense of comfort to know Sarge was there; not that the little animal would be much good against this thing.

The blue creature waved at Archie excitedly. "Don't bee freetened, old manie! Eee em also a Gatekeeper. Eee knows eets secrets. My name is Eethan!"

The blue creature's screechy voice drifted across the heather, his odd laugh causing Archie to twitch. He spilled a large slop of 'all-weather' white paint down the left leg of his tweed trousers. "Aachhh!"

He didn't let it distract him for long, though. His curiosity kindled, he moved closer to the little blue creature, flicking blobs of white emulsion off his leg as he hobbled along. "Keep your distance," he jabbered, holding the paintbrush as though it were a sword.

Eethan grinned, and at the same time, a child's voice sounded from somewhere in the woods behind them.

* * *

Michael was the first to see MacNulty. "Archie!" he called out to the gardener.

But Ephie Blake was the first to see who was with him. She promptly forgot about her hunger pangs and midge bites. Instead, she stared, agog. A blue creature, naked, apart from a small piece of pink cloth, was tittering. And standing next to him was the church organist and occasional gardener, Mr MacNulty. One trouser leg rolled up, he was holding something in his left hand that looked remarkably like a small, dripping dagger.

"I knew it!" shrieked Ephie. "You're all part of some kind of sect. You've lured me here as a human sacrifice!"

As her words echoed round the standing stones, she swayed and fell back into Michael's arms.

"Oh! I can't hold you. You're too heavy!" Michael complained.

Eethan doubled over with laughter as he watched Michael and Ephie fall backwards into the scratchy heather.

"What do you mean, too heavy?" Ephie howled as she scrambled free from Michael's grasp and pulled herself to her feet. "Don't you dare paw me again, Reverend! That's the second time..."

Cathy shook her head. "Paw you? Why would anyone want to do that? Nobody's in the least bit interested in you, you daft woman." Scowling, Cathy stepped round Ephie and marched forward until she faced Eethan. The creature looked different, but she could tell it was still him. "Where's my James?" she shouted. "Have you got him? Is he alright?" Her voice wavered a bit on this last query.

Eethan considered her questions for a moment before saying, "In there." He pointed to the middle of the stone circle before scratching his head and continuing, "No ees not got eem. And yees; at least, ee think so!"

Cathy frowned. "Don't get smart with me, you..."

The group moved closer to the stone circle; all except Archie, who had loosened his sopping trousers and was now attempting to remove them.

"Now what?" Ephie screeched. "This better not be some kind of weird ritual? Get your trousers back on!"

"Twhere cwovered in pwaint you stwupid wuman!"

"Why is he speaking like that?" Jean asked, as she pulled Helen close.

Michael answered for him. "It's his teeth. He lost them this evening."

With a curse that was surprisingly clear despite the lack of teeth, Archie MacNulty pulled his sodden trousers back up again. "Women!" he grumped, swatting the paint off his leg with a clump of heather.

As they stood in the middle of the stone circle, Eethan headed towards the Jesus Rock. When he reached the stone, he put his hand on it and looked out towards Ben Larvach.

Cathy noticed that his hand was beginning to glow.

"Ees might find dees a bit strangee, but Mendel and dee boys need us!" Eethan's wispy voice was barely audible above Patch's constant yelping.

"Shush, Patch!" Michael picked the pup up, but she wouldn't stop barking.

"Shut up!" Cathy screamed at the dog. Patch stopped her yowling instantly. Not because of Cathy, but because the grass under everyone's feet was moving, sloughing away from the rock and soil like a banana peel.

As the centre of the circle detached itself from the bedrock, Eethan muttered a strange word that sounded something like 'sausages'.

He repeated it over and over while everyone else stumbled about, screaming as they crashed to the ground. All but Wee Joe, who clapped his hands and screeched with laughter. "Yippee! Again! Again!"

Patch bolted out of the ring of stones in terror, and in an effort to avoid standing on the mutt, MacNulty fell backwards, rolling out of the circle and cracking his head on a rock.

Shins and elbows banged and bruised, everyone lay motionless on a huge circle of glass. They were suspended high above a fathomless black void, frozen with fright. Patch and MacNulty were nowhere to be seen.

"Everybody needs to geet up and jump up eeen down! Eeh hee!" Eethan's black eyes sparkled in the evening light as he skated from the outer edge of the glass circle to its centre.

Clutching Helen, Jean's eyes widened. "Are you mad?"

"Don't you move an inch!" Cathy shouted. She watched, incredulous, as Ephie shifted her considerable weight in an effort to stand up...

Crack!

"Arrghhh..." they all screamed at the same time.

"Dees es deee best bit!" Eethan stamped his feet on the glass surface and Wee Joe happily copied.

The circular pane, thoroughly weakened, shattered like fine crystal. In one big whoosh, they plummeted down through the Jesus Rocks, spinning and spinning, into the darkness below. Air rushed past their faces, masking Ephie's screams and Wee Joe's laughter, as they were engulfed by the all-consuming abyss.

* * *

Rising to his feet, MacNulty looked around the standing stones in stunned disbelief. He wondered if he might be losing his mind. He ventured forward tentatively in the dim light. "Ish anyone were?" He waited, but there was no reply.

He called out one last time, his voice echoing over the deserted moor, "Favwer Michael!" As he reached for the comfort of his faithful, prize-winning ferret's warm fur, he saw two figures emerge from Tank Woods. It was what passed for the local constabulary: Sergeant Carr and his young trainee, Constable Watt. They had tried to get the better of him for years.

"Don't move an inch, MacNulty!" Sergeant Carr ordered, before beaming down at the young Constable. "We've got the old poacher this time, ferret and all!"

* * *

Far away in the blackness, Cathy Peck managed to push a name from her lips before passing out.

"James..."

21

The Beach and the Hill

In the Forest of Eldane, two cold, wet, tired boys sat on the shale beach by the river. They'd waited over three hours for the barrel containing the goldfish to appear in the water beside them, but it hadn't. Mendel was gone.

Exhausted after their lucky escape from the Centides, they finally gave up, settled down with Bero in a copse of ferns and fell asleep.

Hours later, James felt Bero tense beside him. The retriever issued a low, rumbling growl.

James sat up, immediately hearing what Bero had heard: a distant drumming echoing through the forest.

Bang. Bang. Bang.

He shook Craig, who reluctantly opened his eyes.

James, still half asleep, thought he heard something behind the sound of the drumming, but...it couldn't be. "Mum?" he whispered.

Craig screwed up his face. "Get a grip! It's me, not your Mum, ye numpty! First you say your dad is here and now you're telling me your crazy mum is here too?"

"No," said James, "I was just..."

"You were just talking guff again. Don't worry, keep taking the tablets," narked Craig.

"Listen!" whispered James.

"Yeah," said Craig. He pointed into the dense foliage. "That drumming is coming from over there."

"I could have sworn I heard her voice," James murmured to himself. He pushed up onto his elbows and blinked in the dappled sunlight, sudden realisation crossing his face. "I don't believe it."

"I know. Some alarm clock, eh? It's probably those Osgrunfs again." Craig sauntered over to splash his face in the cool river water.

Bero joined him and began to drink.

James looked round in a panic. "Never mind that. Where's my rucksack? We've been so bloomin' busy looking for Mendel..."

The boys scoured the shale bank, but there was nothing there. James felt close to tears. "It's gone, gone just like Mendel. And now we're totally and utterly—"

"No, we're not!" Craig said firmly. "We're alive and so is Bero, and it looks like you might even find your dad, so don't go getting all depressed on me. I can't stand it when people get all depressed on me. You have to find that talisman thing."

"But I don't even know what it looks like," James complained.

"Well, I reckon this whole thing was staged by the fish. In a weird way we have to trust him. He said you would find the talisman. In fact, he said *it* would find *you*.

"And what are we supposed to do if I find it?" moaned James. "*We* can't do anything. And look!" He pointed up at the sky. Tealfirth looked even sicker than before. It was much redder than the smaller sun, Zalion, and an eery amber hue filled the clearing.

"I reckon we don't have much time in this place," said Craig. "And if you want to find your dad, you'd better start being more positive."

James knew Craig was right, but he couldn't help himself. "I know but..." James froze, an idea forming in his head. "Craig, can you remember your magic word?"

"What? You mean, Greenworm?" From out of nowhere, the green spear appeared in Craig's hand. It glittered in the sunlight, as beautiful as ever.

James pointed to the river and said, "Put it in the water." Craig glanced down at James. "What for?"

"Maybe Mendel will sense it," he explained, growing excited, "or hear it, or..."

"Let's see." Craig lowered the spear's tip into the water and waited. Nothing happened. The rushing river continued on its course, refusing to give up its secrets. Only the distant banging of drums and an occasional birdcall interrupted the silence.

"Duh. What did you expect?" Craig shook his head.

Crunch!

Something stirred on the opposite bank. Something big.

A strange booming call came from the trees across the river, "Ssslathat?"

James took a step back. "Get that spear out of the water."

Craig hesitated, still scanning the opposite bank.

"Quick!" snapped James.

The hackles rose on Bero's neck as the boys edged away from the riverbank one step at a time, keeping their eyes on the shuddering trees. James whispered, "What have you done?"

Craig gave James a withering glance. "What do you mean, what have *I* done? You're the gormless git who told me to put the spear into the water in the first place." Suddenly the whole bank began to vibrate beneath their feet.

"That's definitely not Mendel," said Craig, stating the obvious once again.

They watched in horror as trees a little way back from the other side of the river bent and snapped under the weight of something approaching. More fell, each one closer to the riverbank.

"Ssslathat?" The deep, resonant cry echoed across the

river again.

On the far bank, a large, moss-covered tree splashed into the water, exposing a pair of huge, purple eyes set into a face the size of a small car. James couldn't believe what he was seeing. It looked like one of the Trolls in a book he'd seen at the library. Its fingers were easily the size of James's legs and its teeth were like sharpened stakes. The gnarly skin covering the beast was almost black, with just a few tiny patches of orange. It resembled the crinkled bark of a dying tree.

Cocking his huge, bald head in their direction, the Troll pushed more timber down into the water in order to get a better look at the boys. The gigantic beast was now in full view, yet somehow it still seemed to blend in with the forest.

"Not Ssslathat! Manimals!" The Troll roared, and jerked his head back, sniffing the air.

James remembered the much smaller Swamp Troll doing something similar before it leapt off his mother's roof. He took another step back, feeling sick to his stomach. With each jerk of its giant head, the Troll bellowed a strange cry. "Kak! Kak!" Snapping off a sizable limb from a straining tree, it put a bark-covered foot into the river.

Having by now edged back a good ten yards from the riverbank, the boys slipped and stumbled over clumps of ferns as they retreated further.

"Firetongue!" James shouted, suddenly remembering his word. He glanced down at the red mark on his right palm and waited for the sword to appear. When it did, it immediately began to flick and jerk in the direction of the Troll.

"Do we sit tight or run?" whispered James. Then he gasped. "Bero!"

The Golden Retriever had rushed back down to the

beach to face the creature, barking and growling for all he was worth.

"You stupid dog!" James cried. He could hardly believe what he was seeing. He glanced at Craig. "What does he think he's doing?"

Craig stared at Bero and whispered, "He must think it's some kind of big stick or something!"

"You've got to be kidding me." James crept towards the edge of the bank, his legs shaking fiercely. The Troll was easily thirty feet tall and only needed three steps to cross the river. Seeing Bero below, it laughed, exposing more of its splintered teeth.

"Not Ssslathat. Dinner!" The Troll reached out towards Bero. His long nails were like carving knives. When they were only inches from the old dog, a green spear flew past Bero's brown, floppy ear and sank deep into the Troll's right eye.

"Aaaaaarghh!" As the giant writhed in pain, James lunged forward and grabbed Bero's collar. "Come on, boy!" He tried to pull Bero back up the beach, but the dog dug in, barking and growling more viciously than before as the Troll clawed at his eye in an effort to dislodge the spear.

"Let's get out of here!" James yelled.

Craig hesitated. "He's got my spear!" he moaned.

"Never mind your spear," shouted James. "Just move!"

The Troll screamed in anger and clumped towards them. Clumsily, he thumped his huge club onto the shore, sending sand and stones flying into the bushes behind them.

Before he knew what he was doing, James found himself twisting back. With the effect of Firetongue coursing through him, he ran up the makeshift club until he reached the point where the half-blind Troll's log-like fingers were wrapped tightly around the end.

"James!" Craig yelled hysterically. "Have you gone off your rocker?"

Brandishing Firetongue, James lashed this way and that, hacking through the Troll's fingers until they fell into the river. After a few moments, the club splashed into it too.

The screeching giant grasped at its stump as James twisted away and landed at the river's edge.

"Sssslathat! Ssslathat, my brother. They've blinded me!" The sheer volume of the Troll's voice shook the forest, sending flocks of birds and bats soaring into the air.

Craig pulled James from the water and yanked him back up the beach. "There's another one!"

"What?" James felt dizzy.

Crashhh!

A second Tree Troll thundered through the forest on the opposite bank. "Ashthat!" it bellowed. "Who has wounded you?"

This must be Ssslathat, thought James. He was even taller than his brother and much more menacing. He wore a crest of ferns on his balding head, reminding James of some punk rockers in a photograph his dad had shown him.

Howling his fury, the second Troll threw its massive spear across the river. Luckily for the boys and Bero it fell short, splashing into the water a few feet away and causing a wave of muddy water to drench them.

Bero shook hard.

Reaching his brother, Ssslathat put a hand out to steady him as he screamed a curse across the river. He did not attempt to chase after them, however.

"Do you think he's too scared to cross?" asked James.

"Yeah, right!" Craig frowned and shook his head. "Bero, come!" he commanded, yanking his furry pal away from the river.

Before long all three were running through the Forest of Eldane again, ducking under branches and constantly checking for any pursuing Trolls.

At last, exhausted and shaking, they slowed and bent double.

James had a piercing stitch, but forced himself on up a steep incline, scrambling over patches of bare rock until they were high above the trees. The desire to stop and rest was overwhelming, but a Troll-like wail in the distance made them quicken their pace again. Panting hard, they clutched at ferns, strands of moss, and whatever else they could find to pull themselves up the hill.

Halfway to the top, Craig tugged on James's tattered sleeve. "Wait. Bero can't climb this fast. Slow down!" They waited nervously while Bero caught up.

Eventually, they reached the summit. Turning, they braced themselves for the worst. But there was nothing. No crashing branches or thundering steps, just the distant shouts of the fern-headed Ssslathat and the moans of his wounded brother, Ashthat.

Realising they'd not been followed, James's panic eased. "I still can't believe I can breathe so well," he remarked, half expecting his asthma to seize him the moment the words were out. "It's like a miracle!"

"It's a miracle we're breathing at all after your little stunt back there," said Craig.

"I...I don't know what came over me," said James, leaning against one of the large stones.

"Quite impressive all the same," admitted Craig, giving his friend a grin.

James felt his mouth become dry, but he stood up nonetheless and shouted: "Dad! Mendel!"

"Keep quiet!" snapped Craig, heaving him down by his shirt sleeve.

"What's the point?" said James.

"The point is that you need to cool it. We only have a few hours of daylight left. If you keep shouting like that we'll be lucky to see those out."

James looked round. Denthan's twin suns were setting along the eastern and western horizons and the world was growing dark. "Oh," he muttered. His stomach rumbled as he realised he'd not eaten all day. "Look, there's a city across there." He pointed it out. "That must be Gwendral."

"Wow!" Craig knelt excitedly beside James. "Check out those spires. Think they're made of real gold?"

James squinted. He saw something moving outside the city walls. "Is that grass or...?"

Craig stood up for a better look. "It's not grass, it's living!"

The plain before Gwendral was alive with hordes of weird creatures.

"It's those smelly Osgrunfs," said Craig.

James strained to see. "And look...at the edges! Those are the—" He didn't want to say the word. James shuddered at the sight of the hideous, giant insects that had attacked them earlier.

Craig nodded. "The Centides. Brilliant. Where is that stupid fish when you need him?"

James stared in disbelief. The seething mass of monsters stretched all the way across the huge Plain of Gwendral, from the edge of Eldane to the still sea that shone crimson in the distance. James's shoulders slumped. He felt exhausted from all their running and weak from hunger. "There must be fifty thousand or more of them down there."

Craig grimaced. "How do you work that out?"

"Well, I've been to Hampden Park, to see Scotland in the football..."

"What? Did they get whipped by England again?" Craig smiled down at his friend.

"Hardee-har-har," said James. "Anyway, as I was saying, Dad told me there were more than fifty thousand people there that day." James shrugged, reaching down to pet a delighted Bero.

"There's a lot more than just Centides amongst that lot," said Craig.

They stared at the scene bleakly.

"You still think your dad's here on Denthan, don't you?" Craig suddenly asked.

"You know he is too, so stop trying to wind me up." James flicked a bug off his shorts and looked at his grazed and battered knees. "I know he's still alive."

A sudden breeze ruffled through a canopy of leaves above them and James thought about the prophecy that mentioned the talisman. It was fixed in his memory, so he whispered it out loud. *The talisman moves through ancient leaves and yet, at times, stands still. No Denthan eyes can see it; some say they never will.*

"How can you remember stuff like that?" asked Craig.

James shrugged. "How can a talisman move by itself?"

"Maybe someone – or something – wears it, or has it in a bag or...?" said Craig.

"Maybe one of those Trolls had it," mused James.

"Nah," said Craig, staring at his friend curiously. "Mendel said that it would glow or sing, or something."

James closed his eyes and thought about how much he had suffered since his dad's disappearance. The gossip, meeting Mendel and the complete madness of the whole talisman thing. The worst part, however, was still that he missed his dad so much. He sighed. "What if we don't find Dad in time?"

Craig leaned back against a rock and put his hand behind his head. "Look James, part of me still thinks this is some kind of dream, okay? But it hurts every time I pinch my arm, so it must be real. Anyway, I know you want to believe your dad's in this place, but I just can't see how he could be. I mean, without Mendel. Don't you think he just got fed up with...?"

James preferred Craig's stupid jokes to this. He put his hand up to call a halt to his friend's blabbering.

"Well," pressed Craig, "with your mum going on at him all the time...don't you think he decided he needed some time to himself or...?"

James glared down at his friend. "Mum's been on his case for more than twenty years, so why would he run away now? Besides, she can be kind sometimes." He saw Craig's shocked expression. "She can!" he persisted.

"If you say so." Craig tried to stifle a yawn.

"And what about the compass and the lens cleaner?" James continued.

"Yeah, well, that's funny isn't it?" Craig gazed out at the minarets and towers of Gwendral. "Why would the police have missed the lens cleaner? They searched Bruce Moor for days."

"Well, we found it easy enough," replied James. "Maybe something picked it up and dropped it again."

"Like what?" Craig asked with a frown.

James bristled. "Like a stoat or a weasel. I don't know."

A mischievous grin replaced Craig's freckled frown. "So a weasel stole your dad's lens cloth and then dropped it back beside the Jesus Rocks again? You'd think he'd keep it for his own little weasel binoculars."

"Shut up," snapped James. "Okay, explain the silver compass then. Dad always took it with him when he walked the moor. I never told you, but I found weird footprints up there. One of the prints even had a squashed stoat lying inside it."

Craig looked at him strangely and then brightened. "Maybe a weasel found the compass too. I bet he wanted to use it to find his way about when he went through the gateway. You know, to hunt down the creature who squashed his best mate, the stoat."

"Now you're being facetious," spat James.

"That's one of Mendel's words," said Craig.

"And it means you're being deliberately stupid, so stop it!" James inadvertently gripped his sword a little tighter and twisted its point into the sandy soil.

As an only child, James wasn't used to being pushed to the brink of breaking point, not like Helen and Wee Joe probably were. Pouting, he stretched back and gazed at the vast expanse of glistening water in the distance, determined to ignore Craig.

"You know, it's kind of weird," said Craig, "but right now I've got this really powerful feeling of déjà vu. It's like I've been here before or dreamt it or... oh, I don't know. But I look at the city and I just feel like I've seen it before."

James, still silently seething, hunkered down and stared at the city of Gwendral, with its golden minarets and towering spires. Suddenly, he felt it too. He looked so long and hard that his eyes glazed over and the city blurred into a mishmash of amber, gold and crimson blotches. "Yeah," he whispered, "there *is* something familiar about that city. There shouldn't be, but there is." He yawned too and gathered in his legs until his chin rested on his knees.

Bero and Craig were already sleeping.

22

The Betrayal

Growing increasingly uncomfortable in King Athelstone's tightening skin, Dendralon stood on the highest balcony in Gwendral and took in the scene. The wind swept through his long black hair as he looked beyond the Osgrunfs and Sea Trolls to his Hedra army massing on the southern ridge.

"Sir, I think it's a message bearer."

Behind him, a tanned soldier pointed ahead to a small, flying reptile. Beating its fragile wings hard against the breezes swirling round the citadel, the creature squawked with frustration before landing on the balcony. Dendralon knew the messenger had come from Feldon, the Hedra King, so he waved the Manimal soldier away before removing the tiny note from the reptile's left leg.

Ashthat and Ssslathat, the Tree Trolls, have arrived at our camp as planned. But on the way here, Ashthat was blinded by two small Manimal boys and a yellow beast. Ssslathat wants revenge and can think of nothing else until he gets it. We think the boys may be on the Hill of Dunnad. What are your instructions?

Dendralon scanned the forest until his eyes rested on the rocky knoll. Feeling a frisson of disgust, he stuck his finger into his right eye and peeled back the white Manimal lens. Able to use the full power of his Hedra infrared vision, he focused in on three faint red glows. Was there was a connection between these boys and the meddlesome wizard, Mendel? He had placed a few distractions between the portal and Gwendral, just in case, but he now feared he would have to take more resolute action.

He roared angrily and brought his hand down so hard on the balcony that a small chunk of Manimal skin sloughed off his wrist.

Hearing the cry, the soldier poked his head through the black curtains in alarm, but his master waved him away again.

Quickly, Dendralon scratched out his reply to Feldon.

This is Mendel's doing. Take fifty of your best warriors and kill the boys and any other creature you find in their company. Do not fail.

When he was done, he tossed the reptile off the parapet. It spun down between the spires before righting itself to flap back over the city wall.

Eyes narrowed, he watched the reptile message-bearer glide towards the Hedra camp. When it appeared to be safely on its way, Dendralon looked again into the Forest of Eldane – at the small, rocky outcrop known as Dunnad. Staring at the eerie red light cast over its summit, he thought back to the small boy he'd met in Drumfintley – the one Sleven had failed to eliminate. That would not happen again. This time his Hedra kin would finish the job properly. He would also employ another creature to sniff out this prey. If the boy were to find the Manimal talisman, Mendel might take control of the city. So he would unleash the Wrafnar. It never failed to hunt down and kill its target. He would also put a stronger guard on the portal.

Behind him, the curtains twitched once more. "Sir," the soldier announced, avoiding his King's stare, "the Council is asking for your advice."

Dendralon ensured his voice had a Manimal-like tone as he snapped, "Out of my way." He stepped through the doorway and swept past the red-plumed soldier. He needed to retrieve the crystals and hasten the evacuation of the city.

Time was running out.

* * *

On the southern ridge, above the Plain of Gwendral, the Hedra camp heaved with activity. Huge piles of black-bladed pikes and swords lay ready to be sharpened by the reptilian armourers. Over-laden wagons drawn by large, hideous reptiles creaked along the supply lines, whips cracking as the Hedra drivers steered the beasts through the chaos.

Deep in the centre of the reptilian horde was King Feldon's tent. It sported the bright green flag of the Hedra.

Never far from his king, a Hedra guard called Jal yawned and blinked his yellow-slit eyes. The two setting suns coloured his grey, scaly skin with a spattering of pink and orange highlights. His armoured chest was adorned with a green dragon clutching the twin suns of Denthan. This too glinted in the fading light.

Hunger gripped the giant as he stood, still as a statue, facing the city of Gwendral. It was then, as he tried to quash his appetite, that his wide eyes caught sight of a much smaller, flying reptile, its fragile wings flapping in the distance. It flew unsteadily over the city walls and between the Hedra tents and fluttering flags.

Jal's heartbeat quickened as the reptile flapped closer and closer to him. His tongue flicked from his lips and took in the creature's scent. He glanced round but no-one else had spotted the little flying serpent. It was his for the taking.

As the flyer jerked its way over the guard's head, Jal's long black tongue shot up and wrapped round its left wing. There was a small "Eeek!" as it disappeared into his mouth. Pierced by his poison-laced fangs, the helpless creature was instantly paralysed. It wasn't long before a succession of tiny spines were guiding the meal down Jal's bulging throat towards his large, acid-filled stomach... complete with the message it was carrying.

* * *

Dendralon was delighted to see a real sense of panic building in Gwendral. In the main Council Chamber, Lord Eldane was speaking for the second night in succession. "What conspiracy is this?" he demanded. "The city is completely surrounded. Along with the Hedra to the south, there are now Salt Trolls and Salteths to the West. And as if that's not bad enough, we have Centides and Tree Trolls creeping out of the Forest of Eldane to join the ranks of Osgrunfs and Hedra. Why have all these creatures decided that they should come here? And why now?" He sat down beside his son, stunned by the turn of events.

Since many of the Council members had already left for the tunnels, the Chamber was half empty.

Dendralon stepped onto the serpent-scaled patch of floor before the throne and addressed the remaining few. "Our largest sun is going through a change, nothing more. There are so many superstitions and prophecies, but the real threat is there, in flesh and blood, outside our city walls. Whether we want it to or not, and for whatever reason, our city is going to fall. It is madness to stay! I plan to remain in the city with my elite guards. We will hold off the hordes and allow you all to escape. It would be such a waste to let your own kind perish when they can flee to safety." He stopped and looked directly at Lord Eldane.

Cimerato rose to his feet. "Did you just say, 'your own kind'? Are we to understand that you are not one of us?"

Dendralon cursed himself for making such a stupid slip. "Everyone knows who I am, Cimerato. Why do you pick up on such a triviality? These are times of great pressure. Surely not you, nor anyone here, could doubt that I am your King, Athelstone of Gwendral, son of Elvana and Dersarius, sixty-third Lord of Denthan." Having decided that attack was better than defence, Dendralon watched to see how the remaining Councillors would react. Everyone, apart from Cimerato, bowed his head respectfully.

The young Cimerato changed tactics. "Many of my soldiers will gladly stay and fight to the death if they must. We can use the dragons of Hest against the Hedra."

"What?" Dendralon scoffed. "Twenty ancient serpents that can barely get off the ground? If you want the Hedra archers to have some good sport, so be it!" He tapped his gnarled staff on the stone floor. "Enough, Cimerato."

Yet Cimerato stepped forward. "My father says that you were once a brave and valiant warrior." The whole Chamber echoed with the sound of Councillors' anxious mutterings. "So why do you shy away from this fight?"

Lord Eldane shut his eyes and shook his head at his boy's folly.

"Discretion is the better part of valour, my boy," Dendralon answered, working to stay calm. "At times like these, you must listen to your head and not your heart. With age, you will understand. Wisdom comes with the years that may yet visit you, Cimerato." Seeing the Councillors nodding in agreement, Dendralon pressed home his point. "Time is running out. We didn't see this coming – it has taken us all by surprise. All we can do now is save ourselves and regroup." He turned back to face Cimerato.

The young man was flushed with rage. "Mendel warned

us about Tealfirth. He would have known what to do!" he shouted.

A thin smile lifted Dendralon's dead Manimal lips. Cimerato would not let this go; something would have to be done about him. Dendralon turned away from the troublemaker and closed his white Manimal eyes.

Seconds later, beads of sweat began to drip from Cimerato's handsome face. He grasped his forehead in pain.

"Not feeling well, Cimerato?" Dendralon's tone was conciliatory.

Cimerato dropped to his knees. "You are not the great King Athelstone of old." He clasped his head in his young, scarred hands, gritting his teeth in pain.

Lord Eldane rushed forward to steady his son. He glanced up at Athelstone. "Please! Stop this!"

Dendralon's magic had made Athelstone's Manimal skin flush with vigour and he suddenly looked very powerful. He shook his head in false pity as Cimerato's limp body slumped to the floor. "I did not know Cimerato had a weak heart. Stress is a very dangerous thing." Dendralon studied the Council members, but none looked him in the eye.

Lord Eldane alone shook with fury. "It's not his heart!"

Feeling a stronger energy than he had for a long time, Dendralon wanted to tear off Athelstone's dead skin and reveal who he really was. He wanted to tell everyone how he had captured and killed their pathetic King; and he wanted to turn them all into stone. Instead, he found an inner strength that kept him calm and focused. He dared not harm the old fool. Not just yet. There were still too many Manimals left in the city.

The spines in his throat fell flat to allow him to produce the Manimal voice he'd practiced for so long. "My elite guards are already manning the main gates. I strongly advise that you leave the city before it's too late. I may yet save Gwendral, but the magic I need to perform is new to me and completely untested. We cannot rely on it. I refuse to risk twelve thousand lives, so go!"

Lord Eldane stepped aside as two of the elite guards fussed round his son. "Mendel would have helped you with any magic you needed to perform. Perhaps we should think about bringing him back. Perhaps—"

"Not this kind of magic," interrupted Dendralon. "Perhaps you should take Lady Eldane to safety before it is too late."

Eldane spoke, shakily. "But my son..." Lord Eldane's voice trailed off into a whisper as he made to follow Cimerato, who was being carried from the Council Chamber.

Reading the old man's thoughts, Dendralon said, "Your son will be fine. Now go." Then, turning away, he made for the black curtain that hid the balcony beyond. It was time to summon the Wrafnar.

* * *

Deep in the belly of the city, Cimerato regained consciousness. Far from being in the physician's quarters, he was lying alone in a dank, musty cell. Either some dark magic had possessed their King or, worse still, Athelstone was an impostor, as Mendel had said.

He peered through the barred window and looked down on the creatures filling the plain below. He wondered if Mendel was truly gone forever. He should have supported the wizard when he'd had the chance. Like all the others, he had allowed himself to fall under the spell of the so-called Athelstone. He had feared for his father's safety and had voted for Mendel's banishment.

As a boy, Cimerato had played in Mendel's gardens,

and he remembered now how the old man had smiled whenever he'd asked about some book or strange creature. Always categorising, and often lost in his old manuscripts, Mendel had never failed to listen and answer a curious boy's many questions. Cimerato's eyes filled with tears. He wished Mendel were still able to help them. The old wizard would know what to do. *He* would never have left the city.

With a despondent sigh, Cimerato eased himself down onto the cold floor of the cell and tapped his fingers on the wooden door.

23

The Second Arrival

Michael was the first of the group to open his eyes. The smell of dank church vestry filled his nostrils, and for a moment he thought he had fallen asleep in St. Donan's. It was a belief reinforced when he thought he heard his gardener-come-organist calling his name. Sitting up, he called back, "MacNulty, is that you?"

"Wh...where's MacNulty?" Ephie asked as she straightened her overstretched joggers.

"Wakee, Wakee! We ees here!" Eethan's high-pitched voice echoed gratingly round the tunnel as he paced back and forth in front of them. The little blue man counted the group with a big, toothy grin. "Ees one missing. Thee one weeth the painty brush. Neever mind. Eee must be meant feer something else."

They all shuffled to their feet. They were in some kind of tunnel, at the top of an old flight of stone stairs.

Seeing the steps in the gloom, Jean gathered Helen and Wee Joe in close. "Down there," she whispered, "the roof's collapsed."

"Look at the mess," sighed Michael.

"There must be a thousand tons of rubble," said Cathy, staring at the pile in shock. She shouted down the stairway. "James!"

"Craig?" shouted Helen.

Helen's little voice brought tears to Jean's eyes.

Helen turned to Eethan. "Where's my big brother? Is he here, under the rocks? Are James and Craig and Bero all dead?"

"No, leetle girl. No stinky smell," Eethan said, distractedly.

They seemed to be beside a door of some kind and there was an ancient font a few feet away.

"Now... Let mee see." Eethan moved round the edge of the basin. "Ees a test. But theeres no key! Wee needs the key!" Eethan began to examine the floor, only to discover the letters D.P. carved on the wall.

"You mean this one!" Helen pointed to a small bronze key still protruding from a keyhole at the bottom of the door.

"Yees! Yees!" Distracted from the carved initials, Eethan gave Helen a pat on the back. "Good girlee!" The key hung out of the keyhole at an angle, so he pushed it home. *Clunk!* As soon as he turned it, however, strange noises began to echo up from the bottom of the steps.

"What's that?" whispered Michael.

But his question hung in the air, unanswered.

Something big was moving towards them through the dust and gloom. Eethan glanced once more at the D.P. inscription and shook his head. "Thees door has beeen protected."

Cathy whispered, "Whatever that thing is, it doesn't seem too friendly."

It was one of Cathy Peck's few understatements.

The monster that came into view was a giant of a creature. Red matted fur covered its long-limbed body and a small horn protruded from its forehead. A faint orange glow emanated from the sandy floor of the tunnel and, in the darkness of the passage, tangerine highlights sparkled in its malevolent eyes. The thing struggled to make headway up the narrow section at the bottom of the stairs, growling and bellowing with each step.

"Dees ees bad news," hissed Eethan.

Helen stared at the beast, while Eethan fumbled with

the key. "Look at its eyes! There are four, no *eight*. It has eyes everywhere!"

"Bacckkk..." the creature screeched up at them before falling heavily.

Eethan gulped. "Ee must've turned ee keey the wrong weey. Oopsie!"

Cathy gripped Eethan's scrawny arm. "You mean you made that thing appear?"

Eethan continued to fumble with the key. "Nobodee's perfect, nice laydee! Now help push!"

They all leaned on the door and shoved hard, but it wouldn't move.

"There's a wock jamming it!" cried Wee Joe. The smallest of them, he was able to reach into the hinge and flick the pebble out of the way.

At last, the door started to shift. But the creature, having climbed over the rubble, was now leaping up the stairs ten at a time and getting close.

Cathy gave the blue man an impatient shove. "Quick, Eethan. Open the bloomin' door, or do something about that thing!"

"Eet's a Mertol," explained Eethan. "Ees not an easy beastie to kill. Eees not." Leaving the door, the little man faced the howling beast. Holding his left hand high above his strange, plumed head, he muttered, "Sith tan eech tan!"

A flash of blue light shot from Eethan's hand and hit the Mertol right in the face. Momentarily halted, the red-haired creature stretched its neck and closed its eyes in pain. Pointing a clawed hand at Eethan, the Mertol barked its own charm in return, "Seethh! Baacckkk!"

From an opening on the right side of its cheek, a small red ball shot out and slammed into Eethan's skinny chest. The speed of the attack took Eethan by surprise and he was thrown against the door behind them. The impact was so hard that the door opened even further and now a thin beam of bright sunlight streamed through.

Seeing that the door was moving, the frightened group pushed for dear life, apart from Ephie, who just stood emitting a constant, high-pitched wail. The sound seemed to both annoy and distract the Mertol, which rubbed its eyes and twitched its fur in little spasms.

Another red ball shot from a different 'eye' and smacked into Ephie's mouth with a thud.

"Eeeeeeeee—Uffff!" She immediately froze and then, horrifyingly, started to change. Her skin and clothes began to shine like wet rubber and her body wobbled like a giant moulded jelly. Disjointed, her bottom lip hung down until it bounced off her chest. It looked as though she was melting.

"Ephie!" screamed Michael.

"Hideous!" Jean whispered.

"Weird but interesting," Cathy muttered.

"That's really mean, Mrs Peck," shrieked Helen.

Despite what had happened to Ephie, the group continued pushing on the door. It opened bit by bit until light poured through the gap, temporarily blinding them.

The same light soon fell upon the Mertol and it yelled out.

Squinting, everybody turned, hoping their pursuer would scream and bolt, or turn to stone, but the loathsome beast only blinked and gave an evil, toothy smile. This time, two small black balls shot out from what they could now tell were holes on the sides of its face. The balls burst above their heads, showering them with a fine, black powder.

The last thing they heard was the "Baacckkk" of the creature calling out in triumph.

24

Lost and Found

As the twin suns of Denthan rose over Dunnad Hill, James and Craig slept soundly. Cuddled into Bero, sleep helped them escape their hunger and took them home again to the people and places they already missed so much. James dreamt he was walking over the hills with his dad. His mum was in the dream too, but she was dressed in golden armour, like a warrior queen.

The boys were rudely awakened when their 'pillow' – Bero – shifted.

"Bero!" Craig moaned, still groggy.

By way of an apology, Bero licked their faces, then blow-dried the sticky drool with his stinky dog-breath.

"Yuck, Bero, that's absolutely minging." James grimaced, shading his eyes against the intensity of the early morning light.

"Yep, he's pretty rank," said Craig, "and now so are we. But who cares, eh?" Craig laughed.

"Yeah, but guess what?" James grumbled.

"What?" Craig enquired.

"I don't like smelling like a dead..." James hesitated, looking behind him. "...badger," he finished quietly before asking, "Did you hear that? Something's there." Not giving Craig a chance to reply, James said his special word and the intricately etched sword appeared in his right hand, twitching menacingly. "Get your spear ready!"

Hesitantly, Craig whispered, "Greenworm?" Would the spear come? Was it was still lodged in the Tree Troll's eye?

But it appeared in Craig's hand as commanded.

Surprised it wasn't covered in troll gunk, he tested its weight. The spear still balanced beautifully and shone like polished bronze in the weird Denthan double dawn.

"I thought you didn't feel comfortable killing things in self-defence?" whispered James.

"I don't," barked Craig.

Ready for combat, the boys ventured from their sleeping place. They edged their way down the rocky knoll, hoping nothing in the forest below had seen or heard them. However, they soon realised their path was blocked.

Hundreds of snakes and lizards were using the knoll as a warming site, and not one of them looked friendly.

Craig grabbed Bero by the scruff of the neck and jerked him to a halt. "Whoa, boy. Those might bite."

James stuck his sword into the ground and hunkered down to take a better look. Some of the reptiles had spines covering their backs, others had curved horns on top of their heads.

"They're all awake," said James.

"Yeah... Now what?" said Craig.

Sensing the intruders on the knoll, the reptiles slithered towards the boys, hissing and spitting, their scaly skin glistening in the eerie amber light.

"They're like iguanas without legs," whispered Craig.

"Shut up, Craig. Just get ready to use your spear if you have to," snapped James.

"Has your mum been giving you lessons in tact?" said Craig.

But before James could answer, the squirming mass spread out around them in a deadly arc, moving quicker than the boys had thought possible. Once they were within a few feet, the snakes rose up as one and struck out, forcing them to retreat to the rim of the rocky knoll's sheer face.

James almost lost his footing. "We have to attack now," he shouted to Craig, "or there'll be no way out. They're closing in too fast."

Craig nodded. "Head for that big tree!" He pointed to a huge, misshapen tree off to their left.

Giving each other a subtle nod, both boys leapt forward, swinging their weapons. Longer than James's sword, Greenworm proved the more effective. It swung in deadly arcs, slicing through the moving mass of fangs and scales with barely any effort on Craig's part. Jets of black, serpentine blood spattered the boys' faces and soon a path of wriggling tails and writhing limbs marked their gory progress.

They were almost at the gnarled tree when one of the snakes got too close to James.

"Watch your back!" Craig hollered.

A large black and red cobra, its body as thick as a drainpipe, lunged at James's heel.

Deftly, James sidestepped, but it lunged again, nearly catching hold of his leg. This time James slashed at it with his sword, but his arm was growing tired and he missed. The serpent hissed and attacked again, flicking its barbed tail at Bero. The dog yelped and bounded out of reach.

Craig was busy fighting his own battle, so James had to think quickly. Gripping the hilt of Firetongue tightly in his two hands, he waited for the next strike, spinning round as the snake lunged.

By itself, Firetongue flicked backwards and buried itself between the snake's nostrils, slicing its head in two.

Am I trying too hard? thought James. *Can the sword actually do all the work for me?*

"There's another one!" Craig shouted.

This time Firetongue swung out to slash at a three-headed lizard and there was a gurgle as putrid yellow pus foamed hideously from three headless necks.

Not long after, the snakes began to retreat, perhaps sensing the futility of their attack. Whatever the reason, Bero and the boys were able to make their way down the knoll without any further threat.

When they reached the gnarled tree, Craig came to a stop. He was shaking. "We had to do that, didn't we?"

"Can't hear you," James called, too busy scrambling down the dirt track they'd climbed the night before. He rushed towards the tree.

Craig steadied James as he came to a stop. "I said, I didn't like killing those things!"

"You said, but *I* didn't like the thought of being breakfast, okay?" He shrugged Craig's hand off his shoulder and carried on down the track.

Craig gripped a thick strand of moss as he followed. "He's nearly eighty years old!" he shouted.

"Who is?" said James, tripping over a rootlet.

"Bero is," explained Craig. "He's an old codger in dog years— Oof!" Craig had fallen onto his back and was sliding down the side of the knoll. He grabbed at ferns and strands of moss to try and stop himself. "Help!"

"I think...we've come...the wrong way!" James yelled. He too was flat on his back and gathering speed. The hill dropped away even more.

"Whoa!" Craig fell forward, his yells stifled by thick moss slapping against his face and filling his mouth. Finally, he landed at the bottom of the hill in a heap of arms and legs.

James thudded to a halt a few yards to the left. He was surprised to see Craig licking his lips, delight on his face.

"The moss!" barked Craig. "It's delicious!"

James watched as Craig pulled some more of the grey strands from the nearest tree, and winced as his friend stuffed a handful into his mouth. "Don't be daft. It could be poisonous!"

"Look, I'm starving and I'm having some more." He squeezed some of the grey fibres into a ball. "Here!" he called out to Bero, who had just caught up. "Let's see if you're braver than numpty boy." Craig tossed the ball of moss towards Bero, who caught it in mid-air and gulped it down. "Starving all this time and we were surrounded by the bloomin' stuff," shrieked Craig.

Sheepishly, James put a small piece to his lips. It tasted of water melon. "Hm... Not bad."

"'Not bad'?" said Craig. "It's bloomin' wonderful!"

James gulped down another piece and was soon tearing strands from the surrounding trees as voraciously as his friend.

Half an hour later, and full to bursting, they lay back under another huge, gnarled tree. The Denthan suns had crept a little higher and the air had grown hot and heavy. Gigantic Insects and strange birds fluttered through the canopy above while, at their feet, bright yellow flowers, like overgrown daffodils, grew in clumps between the buttressed tree roots. A purple plant with shiny blue berries helter-skeltered down from the overhanging branches far above.

James let loose a loud burp, feeling satisfied and relaxed for the first time in days. "I wonder how many times the heron's flown by St. Donan's spire now," he remarked, rubbing his full stomach.

"Yeah," said Craig, "and I wonder how many chocolate teacakes our mums have eaten!" He sniggered, already doing the arithmetic. "Last night was our second here, right?" He turned to James.

"I think so, but we did have a kip on the beach for a while..." James began counting up the hours too. There was the trek to the Jesus Rocks, however long in the cave, the hours before first nightfall, their sleep that night, the time when they'd seen the Osgrunfs and Centides, not forgetting the Tree Trolls....

James wrote in the dirt with his finger.

They both sat up at the same time, blurting out the answer. "Thirty-six and a half hours!"

Craig clapped his hands "Ah, but remember Mendel set the loop at thirty minutes, so that makes..."

"Seventy-three teacakes!" They burst into fits of laughter.

"My mum's got to be at least eighteen stone by now!" said James. He could hardly say the words for laughing.

Suddenly his expression sobered and he sat bolt upright. He tugged on Craig's filthy shirt-sleeve. "Did you hear that?"

"What?" Craig was still giggling.

"I thought I heard my mum again. Shouting!" James rubbed his ears as if they had to be playing tricks on him.

"Not again. What is it with you?" asked Craig. "Not that your mum shouting would be unusual, of course. She does nothing else."

"No!" James interrupted. "I heard her shouting 'run.'" He peered through the mass of twisted branches and vines. "I think..."

"I think you've eaten too much of that dodgy moss." Craig stood up and stretched. Then he froze, his hands still high above his head. "Hey, there's something in the ferns!" he whispered. "Look, Bero's wagging his tail at it."

James could hear it now too, a high-pitched chattering. He wondered if he should summon his sword but instead gripped Craig's arm and whispered optimistically, "There must be *some* friendly creatures in Denthan, right?"

The chattering grew louder and the ferns around them twitched. Little sparks of light danced between the fronds. Bero snapped at them. Strangely, though, he continued to wag his tail.

Out of the corner of his eye, James noticed a figure

emerge from the undergrowth. The boys swung round to face a short, balding, yellow-skinned man.

He smiled and bowed politely before saying, "I am Landris." His eyes were completely black except for a pale blue, horizontal slit. James noticed that his thin, angular eyebrows had the same blue tinge. He was dressed in a neat brown jacket and a pair of bottle-green trousers. Smiling again, he asked, "And you are?"

"Eh...James...James Peck."

Craig moved forward and caught hold of Bero's collar. "This is Bero, and I'm Craig."

"And you are lost, are you not?" asked Landris.

"We are," replied James. "And there's someone else who's lost too."

Craig gave James a puzzled stare.

James continued, "That is to say, we've become separated..." He tried to sound calm but his stomach was churning, "...from the person we were with," he finished, already knowing he'd said too much.

"He's in a barrel," Craig explained. "He's a talking fish!"

James couldn't believe Craig had blurted it out like that. He felt a flush of embarrassment when Landris's eyes twinkled.

"Hmm. Well, James Peck, this is not a good place to be chatting, we will go somewhere slightly safer. Then you can tell me all about your talking fish. Come!" With that, he slipped back into the ferns and disappeared.

The ground fell away as soon as the boys ducked into the ferns behind Landris. "Not again!" they cried, but it was too late. Bero barked loudly as they all bowled down an unseen slope. Before long their screams of alarm turned into yelps of exhilaration as they shot down a smooth flume-like slide into the darkness. After a few minutes their descent slowed and all three landed gently on their feet inside a small candlelit chamber. It was decorated with brightly coloured tree roots as well as faded tapestries depicting great battles and weird-looking cities.

The yellow man, Landris, was waiting for them. "Not our most luxurious accommodation," he explained, "but a place where we can talk safely."

Landris used a crooked, glowing twig to light the way. James and Craig followed, wondering what kind of creature he was and where they were. In silence, Landris led them to a much bigger chamber where several other yellow-skinned creatures were standing chattering to each other. They all stopped talking as James and Craig entered.

However, it was Bero who was holding their attention, not the boys. The creatures all stared in wonder at the dog and begged the boys' permission to pat the retriever's soft fur.

"What is it?" a younger version of Landris enquired.

"It's a dog!" Craig declared proudly.

"A dog. A dog..." The creatures repeated the word over and over until their high-pitched babble filled the chamber.

"Silence, please!" Landris shushed them and ushered the boys towards an elaborately decorated door at the back of the hall. When they reached it, he said, "We need to show you something. Young Garlon here found it." He pointed to the creature that had asked about Bero. Garlon grinned and gave them a little wave.

"It was washed up in a small cove," explained Landris, moving behind a low table. He rummaged for something in a drawer. "Garlon is convinced he heard a voice in that place, and when you mentioned a barrel and a talking fish, I thought I might be able to solve your puzzle." He rummaged some more. "Aha!" He held up a strange bag and placed it on the tabletop. The boys stood motionless, watching closely as the yellow man lifted out a familiar object and placed it in front of them.

"The brandy barrel!" both boys shouted at the same time.

James was first to pick it up. He turned the trinket over and peered through the cracked plastic window. "Mendel?"

Landris took a step forward. "What did you say?"

"Someone spoke to me," said Garlon, pressing on, but it couldn't have been Mendel. He was…"

Landris shooshed him. "Let the boys speak."

James peered inside the barrel, then held it to the light. He issued a loud gasp.

"He's not in there, is he," said Craig.

"It's empty," James told him, tossing the barrel over to Craig, who examined it thoroughly.

"What's wrong?" Landris asked, signalling Garlon to stand back.

James turned on the creature. "You couldn't have heard him," he accused, "because he's not in there!" James grew tearful and sat down on a small, wooden stool. In just a few moments, wild exhilaration had turned to complete despair.

"Where is he then?" said Craig, thinking out loud. "He's either been eaten outright, or his little brains have been dashed against the rocks in the river and *then* he's been eaten."

James looked up at Craig through tear-blurred eyes. "Why do you always do that?"

"Do what?" asked Craig, oblivious to the fact that he'd just made matters worse.

"Oh, never mind. Even if Mendel hasn't been splattered against a rock or swallowed whole, the barrel's totally useless now anyway. Look, it's cracked."

James shook his head despondently. When Landris

moved over to touch his arm sympathetically, James could only flash him a tight-lipped smile and pull back, feeling suddenly awkward and stupid.

Landris stepped back too, his blue eyes luminous in the strange light. "Did you say that your friend's name was Mendel?"

"Yes," answered Craig.

Landris and Garlon looked at each other and nodded.

"Sorry," said Craig, "but what do you call yourselves?"

"We are Yeltans," said Garlon, "but are often referred to as Yellow Imps, Woodrands...or dinner, if you're a Hedra," he added with a chuckle.

Landris did not laugh. Instead he became all misty eyed and said, "And the wizard shall return to the Eden Tree." He pointed to an old book in the corner of the room. "That is what it says." He closed his eyes and smiled happily.

"Hey, that's right!" exclaimed Craig, pulling on his friend's dirty sleeve. "Mendel said that if we ever became separated we were to meet him at the Eden Tree."

James fingered the broken barrel. "On the Island of Sen...Sen..." James couldn't remember.

"Senegral," said Landris.

Craig nodded. "Yes, but..." He looked to James. "We need to find something else first."

James wasn't sure if they should say anything more.

Craig pointed to James. "He needs to find a talisman."

Too late, thought James.

"But the talisman is only needed when Denthan is about to be destroyed..." said Landris. He saw the serious expression on James's face.

"But your sun," Craig began, "Tealfirth..." He stared at the two Yeltans and tried to read their expressions. "You don't know, do you?"

Garlon held up his hand and said, "Perhaps once you've eaten and rested a little you may feel at ease enough to tell us how you came to be here in the great Forest of Eldane."

"And," added Landris sternly, "how you came to meet one of the greatest wizards Denthan has ever known."

"But there's no time!" said Craig.

25

The Mertol

An hour before the boys had woken on the Knoll of Dunnad, Jean's eyes had flashed open in sudden panic. "Helen? Joe?" Her voice was groggy as she tried to get her bearings. "Helen! Joe!" She peered through the gloom and saw four cages, all suspended from the ceiling.

She tried to focus, tried to get some idea of what was going on, but the brilliant light to her left dazzled her. A constant rumbling, like the roar of a crowd, was interspersed with strange yells and unearthly screeches, making her wonder if she was still sleeping, trapped in some hellish nightmare. She opened her eyes more slowly this time and saw that she was in a large, open cave.

"I must be dreaming," she groaned, but her thumping head, a foul stench and a breeze on her face all made clear that she was not.

Jean pushed the sweat-sodden hair away from her squinting eyes and desperately tried to comprehend the situation. About a mile into the distance, bathed in a strange unfaltering light, were the golden, jewel-encrusted spires of a beautiful city. She could make out its walls and a jagged outline of minarets. She counted nine tall towers. The biggest, an enormous, white citadel, stretched to the heavens like a giant mast.

"Amazing, isn't it," remarked Michael.

"Michael, where are you?" Jean cried, relieved to hear a familiar voice.

"I'm in the cage behind you. Isn't that the most wondrous sight you've ever seen? Those spires! And the citadel!"

Momentarily distracted by Michael's descriptions of the architecture, Jean snapped out of her trance. "The children!" she cried. "Where are my children?"

"Umm...I'm not sure," admitted Michael, somewhat hesitantly. "But Eethan's over there, tied to a spit, and Cathy is in here with me. I think it's morning, but I'm not sure how long we've been here." Michael's voice sounded weary. "Hours, days..."

"Ees nearer to thirtee hours," bleated Eethan.

"Thirty hours!" wailed Jean.

* * *

Hearing the others, Cathy opened her eyes and sat up. After shaking her head clear, she immediately began to test the cage for weak points. "We have to concentrate! We have to find the kids and what's left of Ephie...if anything."

Cathy's challenge hung in the air unanswered because something had caught Jean and Michael's attention.

Above the city, a grey and white dragon was flapping its monstrous wings slowly and rhythmically. They could hear it barking and yelping like an oversized dog as it flew towards them. Eventually the winged creature reached a long ridge, which they now realised held hordes of reptilian beasts waving black and green flags.

Then, as the giant creature was passing over the hordes, a giant arrow flew up and pierced the dragon's underbelly. Attached to the arrow was a rope, which in turn was anchored to some kind of machine. The attackers wound the rope tight, hauling the convulsing beast screaming and flapping towards the ridge below it.

That was when the stunned observers realised there was someone on the dragon's back. Whoever it was tumbled off as the creature spun to the ground. A blood-curdling cheer was followed by a deafening drumming, and the clash of metal on metal merged with the roars of the baying creatures.

"Helen? Joe?" Jean stared blankly at the patch of sky where the dragon had flapped its last; she began to weep.

"Theey're not here, Jeannie!" It was Eethan, still swinging beneath the spit, desperately trying to free his hands. "Eeee! That's eet!" He had freed one hand and now waved it above his little shock of white hair. "La chee cha sag!" A blue flash of light spread round him and he was suddenly on his feet.

He scrambled up the nearest wall and scuttled across the cave's roof like a spider. "Wee ees lucky," he continued, "that dee Mertol has eaten alreadee!" He pointed to a pile of scaly, flesh-covered bones on the floor.

Jean fainted.

"No ees not the children. Not! These ees Hedra bones." Eethan sounded annoyed.

"What in God's name is a Hedra?" asked Cathy, her voice wavering.

Eethan started opening the cages, choosing to ignore Cathy's question for the time being. Then, after throwing open the last rusty door, he jumped across to a large table and lifted a black saucepan from the debris. He flicked it the right way up and filled it with water, which he poured from a rusting jar. "Wees been sleeping a long time, en already Dendralon's evil ones have filled dee valley. They ees everywhere! Only Mendel and your son" – he pointed a wiry finger at Cathy – "can save our world now." He paused and stuck his thumb up his nose.

"I wish you wouldn't do that," Cathy grumbled before adding, "My son? James?"

"Yees, nice ladee. James has to find the talisman before wees all die." Eethan pointed out of the cave to a very red looking sun. "And I ees still looking for clues!"

"Up your nose?" wailed Cathy. Disgusted, she pushed past Michael and jumped down from the cage. "What has James got himself into?"

Eethan simply chuckled and told them all to come closer. Jean was coming round, and Michael was busy reassuring her that her children would be okay – that they had not been eaten by the Mertol. In the meantime, Cathy confronted Eethan. "Where is my son? Can't you take me to him?"

"Can do a few trickees that Mendel taught me but ee need to find out more." He winked cheekily at Cathy as he dipped his middle finger into the saucepan. A blue flash shot across the water's surface, soon fading to reveal a disturbing scene.

"There!" Michael pointed to the unmistakable figure of Ephie Blake. She'd appeared on the surface of the water. "She's in trouble!"

Jean, fully conscious again, pushed past the reverend to get a better look. "I have to see my children. Where are they? Oh my God..." Jean's voice fell away as the horror of the scene unfolded.

Ephie looked totally worn down. Her rosy cheeks had turned white and her eyes were full of tears. It was obvious she was close to breaking point. "No! No, no!" she cried. "Not again, please! Please, not again!"

Cathy felt a pang of regret. "Poor sod," she muttered.

In the shimmering picture on the surface of the saucepan, Ephie's face drooped and her voice wavered piteously. "You promised me that was the last time. You promised!" Ephie seemed to give up. Then, letting out a small whimper, she began singing, "Two little mice, Tiffy Toffy mice; having adventures and never thinking twice..."

"That's Wee Joe's favourite song!" Jean exclaimed, tears of relief rolling down her face. "He must be making her sing it!"

As the picture panned back, they saw Wee Joe singing along with poor Ephie. They saw Helen too, although she looked as fed up as Ephie.

"Helen hates that song," Jean explained. "She's heard it so many times."

"So the kids are fine," said Michael.

"Yes," whispered Jean.

"How did Ephie survive?" demanded Cathy. "She went all gooey, like she was made of rubber."

"Ees all a Mertol illusion!" Eethan replied, grinning broadly. "Good though, eeh?"

Michael shook his head. "I thought she was dead." He let out a sigh of relief as he stared hard at the kids. "So where are they? I can't tell."

Like a bat, Eethan scampered back up onto the ceiling and looked down at Michael. "Ees another cave. When ee look behind theeem ee can see dee Riveer Levan!"

"Well, I can't see any sign of that ape thing so they must be safe!" said Michael.

"Thank God," murmured Cathy, who had moved in closer to get a better look at the vision in the saucepan. The walls of the children's cave ran wet with damp, and strands of grey moss hung from the ceiling. Behind them, she could see the river.

Deep in concentration, Eethan fiddled with his left nostril. "I ees not sure where de Mertol ees."

Cathy bristled at the sight. "Well, I doubt he's up there."

"Baacckkk!" The horrific cry was followed by the grinding of a heavy stone door being pushed open. Tins and pans clattered at the back of the cave.

"Run!" yelled Cathy through the din. Her shout reverberated out of the Mertol's cave, sending several birds flapping from the trees. She caught the sleeve of her fleece on a piece of armour but managed to wriggle free, leaving it behind.

The Mertol hesitated for a second before picking up a gigantic wooden table. With a terrifying scream it launched it across the cave. "Baacckkk!"

The table smashed into a huge stalactite, shattering it into a hundred pieces. The impact showered the fleeing group with dust and limestone.

Coughing and screaming, Cathy, Jean and Michael ran out into the suns' red light.

Eethan, however, remained in the cave. Scampering across the roof, above the Mertol's head, he made a dash for the open door at the opposite end.

Outside, Jean and Cathy chased after Michael, down the tree-covered slope towards the valley. Behind them the Mertol screamed again, but then turned unexpectedly and leaped back into his cave. Cathy supposed the beast had doubled back to chase Eethan.

26

Rafts and Rations

Eethan knew that magic was always drawn to magic, so he tried to remain as still as possible. Below him, the Mertol searched the cave. Creeping along the litter-strewn floor, the creature's heel knocked over the saucepan. The enchanted water splashed onto the surface, causing sparks and flashes of electric blue to swirl round the Mertol's feet.

"Baacckkk!" the beast called out again, stumbling over the debris and crashing into one of the swinging cages.

Clinging to the vaulted roof, Eethan scampered through the open door and into a secret passage. In seconds, he was able to put a good distance between himself and the Mertol and soon arrived at a dank, moss-covered cave.

"Eethan!"

It was Ephie, her bloodshot eyes wide with relief.

With a flick of his wrist the door on their cage sprung open and the captives leapt free. Wise enough to keep quiet – even Wee Joe – Ephie and the kids followed Eethan out of the shadowy cave. The dark green river oozed past them as they made their way along its slippery bank, ducking through the lacy veils of moss that hung from the branches above. They walked for several hundred yards before Eethan guided them into a clump of ferns.

Eethan motioned to them as he pointed to the ground. "Everyone sit still. Don't ee move, make sounds or singy songs."

Ephie wiped the sweat from her brow and patted Wee Joe on the back. "Don't worry. No singy songs. We promise. Right?" She smiled weakly at Wee Joe, who stuck his tongue out and made a farty sound. "Pthuuuuuw!"

Ephie's brow wrinkled, then she leaned across to whisper to Eethan, "I'm so glad you came when you did. That thing was very gentle with the children, but—"

"Dee Mertol doesn't harm little ones," Eethan interrupted with a grin. "No, neever. Only eets *you* for dinneer, Eeeephie." The little blue man chuckled at her horrified expression, then disappeared back into the bushes.

"It's Ephie, not Eeeephie," bleated Ephie, "whatever you are." She sighed and looked round, still trembling from their ordeal.

"Eeeephie. Eeeephie!" Wee Joe called out, adopting Eethan's pronunciation. She fumbled frantically in her deep overcoat pockets for some more tablet to shut him up. She had to find some! She was willing to give him the whole lot - anything to stop Wee Joe drawing the Mertol to their hiding place.

As she dug about, she wondered if the others - especially Father Michael - were okay. She didn't know why, but she was beginning to change her mind about the new priest.

She found what she was after and shoved some tablet into Wee Joe's sweaty, grasping hands. She then passed some to Helen.

Blessed silence descended as the kids stuffed their mouths with the sweet flakiness.

* * *

Splashing through the river that lay below the Mertol cave, Cathy hoped the water would cover their tracks. She could see that Jean was struggling against the weight of her sodden mohair cardigan. "Take that bloomin' thing off!" she snapped. But just as she was going to help her with it she heard a familiar voice.

"Psssst!"

Eethan was standing on the riverbank, waving them over.

Exhausted and soaked, they followed Eethan into the forest without a thought of where he was leading them. Their brains were too numb.

"Mum!" Helen jumped from a clump of ferns and threw her arms round Jean's neck.

"Helen! Joe!" cried Jean in stunned delight. All three burst into tears as they clung to each other.

"My back is killing me!" Michael complained, his eyes screwed up tight in pain as he shuffled across to a patch of grass to sit beside Ephie.

Cathy shook her head and lay back on the damp grass. "Men!" she sighed as she stared up at the patches of blue beyond the canopy, her mind drifting to thoughts of James and the man who had deserted them in Drumfintley more than three weeks earlier. A terrible emptiness took hold of her.

All men are pathetic, she decided. *They never stop moaning and are useless when they fall ill or have aches and pains. At least I won't have to listen to David moan about his heartburn or his back or his lack of sleep.*

A small tear rolled down her left cheek, but she quickly wiped it away before anyone noticed.

In the distance, they could still hear the muted screams of the Mertol. "Ee thinks the Mertol's having a bad day," Eethan tittered. "Ee'll be wary of Hedra archeeers."

Hearing this, Cathy snapped out of her daze, remembering what had happened to the dragon. She sat up and pointed at Eethan. "Never mind the Mertol, let's focus on the important things. When are we going to find my son? What do we do now? And..." Cathy stopped to steady herself against a small tree, "...what is there to eat around here? I'm *starving*."

Eethan simply glanced once over his shoulder at her and answered all three questions in his sing-song voice: "Soon. Build a raft. And this!" He stood up and offered her some moss, a cheeky, needle-spiked smile spreading across his leathery face.

Cathy jumped up and grabbed Eethan by the throat.

Michael stood up. "In God's name, Cathy, leave him alone!"

Cathy glanced sideways at the reverend and saw he was shaking with rage. Apparently, the man had a bit of back-bone after all.

"No violence in front of my children, please!" said Jean, pulling the kids closer to her. She shot Cathy and Michael an accusatory stare.

Cathy let go of Eethan's neck and whispered, "Pathetic. You're all pathetic." Free from her grip, Eethan clutched his throat and coughed. Undaunted, he managed to blink out another smile. "Ees nice. Try some." He waved the moss at Cathy again, but not for long. Ephie snatched it from Eethan's fingers and stuffed it into her mouth.

"Mmmmm. It's delicious!" Her plump cheeks regained some of their colour and she sighed in ecstasy. "It's not tablet, but..."

"Mossgeld," explained Eethan. "Eees full of veetameens, so eet ees."

"Yummy!" said Wee Joe, pulling a strand from the nearest tree.

"It tastes like melon candyfloss!" cried Helen, already chewing on the sticky strands. Soon they were all pulling strips of Mossgeld from the trees. Eethan disappeared for a moment, returning with a cup-shaped leaf filled with water, which they passed round. Only Cathy remained sitting, her back to a tree, staring blankly into the distance.

It was Michael – forever the peacemaker – who crouched beside her and offered some water, but she didn't even acknowledge him. Instead, she continued to look ahead into the gloom of the forest, oblivious to all, alone in the prison of her rage.

After they'd eaten and rested, Eethan explained what they needed to do. "Wees have to build a raft and go upstream, away from all dee bad things. Wees have to start now. I theenk Mendel will take dee boys to dee Eden Tree and that's furtheer up dee Reever Levan from heere! Eet will all be pointless, though, if your boy James does not find dee talisman."

Cathy threw her head back with a sigh and said, "My James can't even find his socks in the morning, never mind some tal…"

"Talisman," said Eethan.

"Whatever," snapped Cathy. "So get used to it, we are all dead already."

Jean, Michael, Ephie, and Eethan all stopped what they were doing and stared at Cathy.

"What?" she blasted.

With some encouragement from Eethan they wandered back, dejectedly, to the river's edge and began gathering the necessary logs and vines to build the raft.

For a whole hour Cathy continued her sulk and did nothing to help.

It was Helen's voice that eventually cut through her angry thoughts. "It's ready, Mrs Peck. Come and see it. We're all waiting on you."

Cathy looked up to see them arranging themselves on the raft. Moored to an overhanging branch, it bobbed in the green water. Ephie sat at the front of the craft with Michael, while Jean and Eethan manned the rear.

Befuddled, Cathy took Helen's small hand and walked down to the beach.

Helen addressed the tight-lipped onlookers. "I think she's sorry." She smiled up at the blank-faced Cathy. But Cathy had neither the will nor the energy to acknowledge the little girl.

There was an uneasy silence as the raft moved out into the river. At first it led them the wrong way, drifting them back towards the Mertol's cave in a slow current. However, they soon got their rhythm going and the makeshift paddles propelled the craft upstream, further into the forest.

Eethan beamed. "Ees not too deefeecult, eh?"

They soon passed close to the underside of a rocky knoll.

"Ees called Dunnad," explained Eethan.

Cathy was just about to tell Eethan to quit yapping when she felt a tingle down her spine. It caused her to gasp. "James!" she called, blinking up into the morning light that flickered down through the canopy.

"Why did you shout on James, Mrs Peck?" Helen enquired.

"Um, no. It was nothing," said Cathy, suddenly annoyed with herself.

It felt cooler beneath the overhanging branches as they paddled deeper into the shadows of what Eethan told them was the Forest of Eldane. Wee Joe's high-pitched voice echoed out over the green waters, "Two wittle mice, Tiffy Toffy mice, having adwentures and never finking twice..."

27

The Last Supper

Deep beneath the Forest of Eldane, Landris was keen to exchange information with the boys as soon as possible. James overheard him giving instructions – *get the elders, prepare a special meal, put extra guards on watch.*

Garlon caught James's attention and then waved Craig and Landris over to a quiet corner. "We have found some clothes. They might be something to do with your quest, as I know of no other creatures that wear your apparel."

James looked perplexed.

"He means you've got terrible fashion sense," said Craig.

James straightened. "Maybe it's Dad!" He saw a flash of irritation in Craig's eyes.

Garlon and Landris led them to the chamber where they'd first entered the Yeltan caves. Mendel's broken barrel sat on the desk, as it had earlier. Walking past it, Landris stretched up to retrieve a small cloth bag from a high shelf. "I hope you are prepared," Landris said gravely to James. The Yeltan tipped a black fleecy jacket onto his desk.

James stared down at the familiar item for a second, then turned to Craig. He couldn't speak.

Frowning, Craig picked up the jacket. "It's your dad's alright."

"Yes," whispered James. "I think he had it on the night he disappeared." James stared at Craig. "*Now* do you believe he's here?"

Craig shrugged. "Who knows."

Ignoring Craig, James tried to fathom Landris's strange expression. "Where did you find it?" he breathed.

"We found no trace of your father," Landris replied. "Only the jacket, but..." He turned to Garlon.

"They were found at the entrance of a cave," said Garlon. "A Mertol's cave."

James and Craig didn't know what a Mertol was, but it sounded bad. Bero licked James's hand.

Landris continued, "The Mertol is a fearsome creature that ranks Yeltan as one of its favourite dishes."

"You think it's eaten his dad, don't you?" Craig blurted.

Landris and Garlon said nothing.

James felt sick, then suddenly brightened. "Wait a second...Mendel told me he was certain my dad was still alive! He said we still have a connection."

"That was a few days ago now," said Craig, "but...but let's not get too gloomy about all this. It's a start."

James felt his temper boiling to the surface. "I hate you sometimes, Craig."

"Dendralon's the one you should hate," said Craig.

Dendralon's name caused Landris to gasp. "Why do you say that name?"

Craig sniffed. "Well, it was Dendralon who banished Mendel. Neither of us would be in this mess if it wasn't for him."

"He's disguised as a Manimal King," added James.

"King Athelstone? Are you saying that the king is an impostor?"

"Yup," answered Craig.

"You must tell us everything," instructed Landris urgently, beckoning Garlon closer.

* * *

Landris and Garlon wailed like a pair of strangled cats

as James and Craig finished their explanation about the imposter Dendralon and the imminent explosion of their sun, Tealfirth. "Whaaa! Noooooo!"

"Look," James interjected, "you said you would take us to the Eden Tree. So why don't we go there now?"

The Yeltans still looked distraught. "We must tell the Manimals about Athelstone. This makes perfect sense, *perfect* sense."

Garlon and Landris babbled to each other in a high-pitched language the boys could barely hear. Bero seemed to hear it though. Whenever they began their strange mutterings, his tail wagged.

Finally, Garlon calmed down a bit. "The Athelstone of old would never have banished Mendel. We always knew this. To think that Dendralon is behind this. If he has truly returned, we are in grave danger. He is probably the most powerful wizard ever. It took a hundred years to defeat him the first time around."

"Well that's a pity," remarked Craig. "Because according to Mendel we've got about a day and a half."

The Yeltans' wailing began over again: "Whaaaa! Oooooo!"

"Nice one, Craig," sighed James, covering his ears. "If we ever make it out of here, you should really consider joining the Diplomatic Service."

Ignoring him, Craig was about to say something else to the Yeltans, but James, deciding his friend had said more than enough, gave him a swift kick.

"Argh! Owww..."

The wailing Yeltans, who must have thought Craig was commiserating with them, hugged him and wailed even louder.

Other Yeltans had gathered at the doorway by now, drawn by the commotion. James tried to get Landris and Garlon's attention. "We have to get going!" he yelled.

"There's no time to waste!"

After another few minutes the terrible noise died down. Landris shook his head. "I'm sorry James, but we cannot leave before we eat."

"Before you eat?" exclaimed Craig, a look of bewilderment on his face. "We need to leave *straight away.*"

Landris heaved a shuddering sigh. "I know it must seem strange to you, but it is our way: food, talk, then action. Besides, you said you have to find the talisman?"

James frowned. "Well that's going to be easier said than done. I don't even know what it looks like."

"But it glows in the dark, sings and moves through the trees," said Craig.

James gave him a withering glance.

Craig took hold of Bero's collar and addressed Landris. "It might be better for us to head off and hope we find the talisman on the way. Or find Mendel, who can help us find the talisman... It's just that, with Mendel being a fish..."

"A very small goldfish in very a big river," continued James.

Craig screwed up his face. "...and with the sun about to..."

"We heard you the first time," sighed Landris. "As we said..."

"Food, talk and then action?" said James.

"Exactly," said Landris. "It's the Yeltan way."

James felt a warm knot of anger building in his stomach. "Look! We do not have time to sit and eat anything!"

Craig took a step back and stared at his friend.

"Everything we do," said Landris, still maintaining a calm tone, "is based around protocol. We have a way of doing things that may seem strange to you but..."

"Can't we eat once we get to the Eden Tree?" said Craig.

"I'm afraid it's out of the question," said Landris.

"So," said James, trying his best to stay rational, "even though you know your world is about to blow up, you are going to sit down and have some dinner?"

"Exactly," said Garlon, with a friendly but very annoying smile.

"Un-bloomin-believable!" sighed James.

Craig shrugged.

"The banquet is ready in the great hall," said Garlon. "Come."

As they moved off, Craig caught hold of James's arm and whispered sharply in his ear. "I don't get it either. One minute they're crying their eyes out because they think they're all going to die, the next they have to eat?"

"Well, it better be a ready meal," said James.

"Somehow, I doubt that," groaned Craig.

As they set off towards the great hall, James wondered if maybe Landris knew more about Mendel's banishment than he was letting on. Had he been part of the group that had made the decision?

On their way deeper into the labyrinths, James noticed a large room lined with an assortment of golden spears. He nudged Craig, who asked Landris what it was. It was their armoury, Landris explained as he stopped in front of a large tapestry, which now caught James's attention.

"What do those pictures show?" James asked.

Landris turned round. "This tapestry depicts the arrival of the Dragons of Hest almost three thousand years ago. And that..." – Landris pointed to a blue-cloaked figure seated on the back of a white dragon – "...is Mendel."

James wished he hadn't asked. This was only going to slow things down even further but he reached out and touched the woven cloth, tracing the bumps and fibres with his fingertips. He stared hard at the blue-cloaked figure, but there was just not enough detail. Mendel was only a tiny part of an enormous landscape.

The epic scene depicted the nine towers of Gwendral surrounded by a host of different-coloured dragons. They looked as though they were chasing away a massive army of grey-skinned reptilian creatures.

Landris said, "The Hedra fled, disappearing into the Southern Marshes."

Standing further back, Craig noticed a smaller blue figure sitting next to Mendel, his hand raised above his snow-white hair in an odd gesture.

Garlon too traced his fingers over the tapestry. "The creature you see beside Mendel is Eethan Magichand. He was a powerful sorcerer and is still worshiped by our race. Mendel has already saved us once. Let us hope our great wizard can do it again."

As they took their seats in the great hall, James's chest tightened with nerves as it was announced that they would be feasting on steamed Radnit fish, grilled rootlets, golden-spotted mushrooms and purple Mossgeld. He noticed an intriguing array of little drinks laid out in concentric rings across the table. Yellow, green, and even black liquid filled the delicate crystal goblets and the Yeltans seemed to pick certain colours to go with certain courses.

Craig was the first to try one. "Gonie huv some, James!" announced Craig, in his most annoying, phoney Scottish accent. "Ish wan tastes jist like bubble-gum! Try it!"

James shook his head in despair at his friend's mimicry, but Craig ignored him and slid over a small glass containing a thick yellow liquid.

James cautiously took a sip. He shivered as the drink filled his nose and mouth with flavours. "You're right. And creamy chocolate too. Whoa! It's delicious!" Reaching for more, he soon caught up with Craig, drinking four in a row.

"So what's this called, Landris?" Craig held up a glass

of the bubble-gum drink and started to giggle.

"That one is Lugpus," answered Landris.

"What-pus?" Craig cried, then laughed loudly, his eyes tearing up.

Landris explained, "We harvest it from the ears of an animal called a Yukplug, then leave it to cool in the river for at least two days."

By now, James was in fits of laughter too. "That's totally disgusting!" he guffawed, spitting some of the liquid onto the table.

"James! Manners!" Craig patted his friend on the back as he roared and slapped his knee.

It didn't take long for the boys to realise that the laughter was becoming painful.

Landris signalled to Garlon. "I think they've had a little too much." Garlon nodded then looked down the table at the two helpless boys, who were shaking and unable to get up. Lying on his back, Craig did a good impression of Mendel's bubbly fish voice by pinging his lips and attempting to talk. "Who's a pwwwetty bwwoy wen? Who's a pwwwetty bwwoy?" Garlon laughed and, moving closer, produced a crumpled cloth bag from his red belt. He nipped a pinch of yellow powder from the bag and blew it straight into their faces.

Instantly, their laughter stopped. Somewhat bemused, they got to their feet and picked up their chairs. James looked round, expecting to see accusing stares or outrage, but there were neither. Everybody continued talking and eating as if nothing had happened.

Landris addressed them. "It does that," he said quietly, "it makes you giggle, but if you take too much, you laugh and laugh until you take some anti-mirth powder."

Raaaaaar!

Instantly everyone at the table stopped eating and drinking.

"What was that?" asked Craig, a small snigger escaping before he managed to cover his mouth.

Landris shouted commands to Garlon and the rest of the Yeltans and then caught James by the sleeve. "Go with Garlon!"

Raaaaaaar! This time the frightening cry was much closer.

"It's a Wrafnar," said Garlon. He ushered the two boys down a steep slope. "They are impossible to kill."

"What is it doing here?" panted Craig. He was still unsteady on his feet.

"They are assassins, killers. They work for dark wizards." He stopped beside some kind of pen and looked up at the angry sky. "Dendralon must want you dead after all," he said.

"Why?" moaned Craig.

"Because you alone can stop his madness," said Landris. The older of the two Yeltans skidded to a halt beside them. "If you are truly the one meant to find the talisman, he will try to kill you."

"Quick," gasped Craig, "call on Firetongue."

Both boys said their magic words.

"Nothing," said James. "The magic words aren't working."

"Your voices," explained Garlon. "They have been altered by the Yukpus."

"For how long?" asked James.

"Three or four hours," Garlon said.

Landris nodded confirmation.

Raaaaaaar!

A cluster of trees to their right shook violently as a monstrous creature stepped into view. It was a good twenty feet tall with three arms on each side of its body. It stood on two spiny legs and its head was V-shaped, with a large single eye in the space between the V's two arms.

The eye spun rapidly then stopped suddenly. Four of the six limbs pointed at the boys.

"Get into the Yukplug pen!" Landris commanded.

Several Yeltan spears found their mark, thudding into the creature's insect-like carapace, but that didn't stop it. It kept approaching, yanking out the spears and growling deeply as its hard skin repaired itself.

"We can't kill it, but you might be able to outrun it if you take a couple of Yukplugs," said Garlon. He pointed across the pen at some stables.

"I don't understand," wailed James.

Landris bounded over the small picket fence and raced towards the stables.

The Wrafnar lifted off the ground, a pair of membranous wings whirring into life. Bero barked and growled as it moved closer.

Five or six Yeltans ran towards the creature and threw more spears, but the Wrafnar caught the missiles in its arms and tore them to pieces.

"Keep back!" instructed Garlon.

Another group of Yeltans retreated just in time. The Wrafnar sprayed a thick, noxious liquid at the spot where they had stood. It burnt everything to a crisp.

"Run!" yelled Garlon.

James and Craig bolted after the young Yeltan, still clutching Bero's collar. They ran across a paddock deep with wood shavings, towards the stables.

Landris appeared with two animals that looked like Woolly Mammoths crossed with ostriches, thickly brown-haired but with long necks covered in feathers.

"The Wrafnar won't harm us if we don't engage it," he told them. "You must ride these Yukplugs away from here as fast as you can."

Craig was mesmerised. Including its head and neck the Yukplug stood some six feet high on its thick scaly legs.

Its long ears flickered as Craig drew closer. A single white horn peeked through its woolly mane and wet nostrils flared and dripped yellow blobs of liquid onto the sand. Craig jumped up onto the Yukplug's back as the Wrafnar roared above the clearing.

"James, take care of Fledha, she's the oldest Yukplug we have," said Landris.

James glanced between his slightly decrepit-looking Yukplug and the Wrafnar, which had dropped into the pen with a loud thud. With another roar, it leapt forward.

Craig was thrown from his mount, a long hairy arm narrowly missing his head.

Landris and Garlon scattered as it scuttled after them, jabbing the ground with the knife-like tips of its six arms.

"Craig!" yelled James, kicking his Yukplug into action. It raced over to Craig and dodged another swiping limb, enabling James to hold on to its horn whilst he grabbed hold of Craig. As he did, however, there was a loud shriek. James got such a fright that he slid backwards off the Yukplug and thumped heavily onto the woodchips.

The breath was knocked from his lungs and he felt something hot in his hand. A ringing soon filled his ears.

The screaming Wrafnar jumped over the two boys and poised to strike with a pair of fangs that had dropped down from its bulky head. They glistened in the crimson light filtering into the glade, black venom dripping onto the ground either side of them.

"Roll!" yelled Craig.

They both moved a second before the fangs sank deep into the ground, showering them with an arc of damp woodchips.

James glanced at his hand. The Yukplug horn was glowing. His fingers were bright red, almost see-through with the sheer intensity of the light. Another ringing blast echoed out of the Yukplug horn and caused the Wrafnar to stop.

It drew in its dripping fangs and thrashed about, the deadly points of its arms jabbing deep into the earth all around them.

"James!" yelled Craig, tears rolling down his cheeks. His shirt was pinned to the ground and he couldn't move. "The Yukplug horn! Maybe it's the...!"

James rolled out from underneath the Wrafnar and stood up. Suddenly, Mendel's voice seemed to be everywhere: "*The talisman moves through ancient leaves and yet, at times, stands still...*"

The Yukplug horn, thought James. *"...No Denthan eyes can see it; some say they never will."*

The talisman had been there in the ancient forest all along, but the Yeltans had never realised.

James tried to focus. Yeltans were appearing from everywhere around the pen. They looked on in amazement.

Feeling a surge of energy similar to the power of Firetongue, James held the Yukplug horn in front of him like a weapon and yelled, "By the power of the talisman I command you to return!"

The Wrafnar shrieked and tried to fly, but its wings crumpled as if singed by a giant flame and it crashed back to the ground.

"Return!" repeated James, his whole body shaking.

This time the creature roared in frustration, its single eye spinning like a top, its limbs thrashing this way and that, flailing against the ground. A loud, distracting chorus of angelic song filled James's head.

Then, with a rush of wind that shook all the trees around the pen, and with a great crash of thunder, the Wrafnar disappeared in a blinding flash of white fire.

James yelped and dropped the Yukplug horn, blowing on his fingers. "Craig?" His best friend had been directly under the Wrafnar. "Craig!"

"You did it!"

James quickly rubbed his eyes on his sleeve and saw Craig walking towards him, a huge rent in the arm of his shirt.

"You killed it!"

James grabbed Craig and shook him. "Are you alright?"

"Yeah. Just a scratch," Craig coughed.

Landris and Garlon strode back into the pen and gathered up the Yukplugs' reins.

"I doubt you've killed it, James," said Landris, "but you've sent it back to whatever dark hole it came from." He looked up at the dying Denthan sun, smiled and said for all to hear, "James Peck, you have found the talisman. You've given us all a chance to live through this nightmare."

A thousand Yeltan voices roared out in rapturous unison. "James Peck! James Peck! James Peck!"

Landris and Garlon raised their fists and joined in.

Craig smiled at his best friend, but then winced and dropped to one knee.

Landris immediately lowered his arm and the glade fell silent again. "He's been poisoned."

James knelt and cradled his friend, watching him shake and sweat.

"It must have nicked me," groaned Craig.

James, still holding the talisman, placed the charm on his best friend's chest, unsure what to expect but desperately hoping it would have some effect.

With a sharp breath, Craig suddenly stopped breathing and closed his eyes.

"A wound from a Wrafnar never heals," whispered Landris.

James didn't know what to do. "No! Craig, wake up!" The silence engulfed James, chasing every idea out of his head.

"Ask the talisman to save him!" urged Garlon.

It had all happened so quickly with the Wrafnar – his words, the way he had held the talisman.... But now... He stared at the curved Yukplug horn in his hand and saw his tears drip onto its glowing surface.

Bero was whining, nudging Craig's still body with his wet nose.

"Save him," whispered James. "Please save Craig." He closed his eyes and felt the talisman pulse. A single note faltered and then strengthened. It sang out over the glade and was soon amplified by a thousand Yeltan voices copying it.

James opened his eyes and saw the talisman blazing brightly on Craig's chest. A blinding beam of light shot into the sky and seemed to go beyond even there...

28

The Darkening Sky

High in the citadel of Gwendral, standing alone beside the great Scales that would tip the balance in favour of his own Hedra race, a blast of light and power threw Dendralon back against his ivory throne.

Forcing himself to his feet, the Hedra wizard realised the Scales had broken into a thousand pieces. Distraught, he tore the Manimal flesh away from his scaled face and narrowed his yellow reptilian eyes, then staggered onto the balcony. In a loud and unmistakably Hedra voice he wailed, "Mendel!"

He should have killed the Manimal wizard when the interfering old fool had first suspected he wasn't Athelstone. Now he knew that Mendel had found a way back to Denthan.

He stared out over the wailing armies and beyond, to the Forest of Eldane. He closed his eyes and tried to find a way through his rage. "There must still be a way..."

His eyes snapped open and a low gurgling hiss of satisfaction formed at the back of his throat. "Yessssss... I can still collect the crystals, and then repair the Scales with the talisman; for that is what has caused this setback. Only the talisman of Denthan can have banished a Wrafnar. Only *it* can have destroyed the great Scales of Gwendral."

Dendralon rose to his full height and picked up his gnarled staff.

"But what it has destroyed it can repair! The talisman can *rebuild* the Scales and bring *back* the Wrafnar. The boy..." – Dendralon could feel the Hedra magic pulsating through him – "...the boy they call James Peck... The very same child I met before I found Sleven. The Yeltans chant his name. They shall pay dearly for this."

He smiled and let the needle-sharp spines in the back of his throat click together in anticipation. He raised his staff high and yelled, "I call on the dead! The winged dead. The Keresi! Come back from the void and return to blot out this dying sun. Seek revenge for your Hedra kin. Bring me the boy James. Bring me the boy James Peck!"

With a massive judder of stone on stone, the ground beneath the Citadel opened up. Manimals ran for cover as the cobbled courtyard exploded in a deadly shower of rock and earth. Then, from the dark void, a deadly cloud of glistening black wings erupted like a whirling tornado. More and more reptiles poured out until the sky turned black and a great shadow covered the plain of Gwendral.

* * *

Wee Joe stopped singing and Eethan stood up on the wooden raft.

Cathy saw the concern on the blue man's face. She saw him bow his head and begin to chant over and over. "What is it, Eethan?"

Without their paddling, the raft started to drift back downstream.

"Ees good and bad," said Eethan.

"What's the good bit?" asked Michael, anxiously.

"Yes," said Ephie, "don't look so...so alarmed. You'll frighten the children."

Eethan looked straight into Cathy's eyes. "James has found the talisman of Denthan."

"What does that mean?" asked Helen.

Eethan forced a smile. "Eet means that Dendralon can

be stopped."

"Who?" asked Michael.

"He ees bery bad creature," said Eethan.

"Okay," said Cathy, impatiently. "Now what's the 'but'? I can feel a big 'but' coming along" – she glanced at Ephie – "and I'm not talking about you."

"How dare you!" squawked Ephie. "I—"

"Shut up!" hissed Cathy. She suddenly stood up on the raft and everyone had to grip the sides as it wobbled and tilted.

"What are you doing?" said Jean.

But Cathy ignored them all and jumped straight into the water. The river Eldane came up to her waist as she waded across to the bank.

"She's really lost it this time," said Jean.

Michael paddled to keep the raft stationary, his eyes firmly fixed on Cathy. "No, she's found something."

"Is it one of the boys?" gasped Jean.

Cathy stooped down and snatched up a sodden green rucksack. "It's his!" She turned to the rest of the group, a manic look on her face. "It's James's rucksack!" She waded back towards the raft and pointed at Eethan. "Where is he? Where is my James?"

It suddenly grew very dark, as if someone had closed a very heavy curtain.

"No," replied Eethan, "Ee dees not know whee thee boys are. But Ee thinks that *they*" – he pointed skyward – "do".

An endless cloud of flying creatures filled the heavens, so tightly packed that they doused Denthan's twin suns. It sent all the strange animals of the forest into a cacophony of wails and screams so intense that the raft's occupants had to cover their ears.

Long shadows crept out from the tall trees that surrounded them and soon turned the river as black as any night.

Cathy stood in the middle of the river, lifted the dripping rucksack high above her head and shouted as loudly as she could over the terrifying din, "JAMES!"

* * *

Under the waterlogged trunk of a long-dead tree a glimmer of gold dared to ease free for the first time. With a swish of its tail the goldfish swam downstream, letting the current take it on its reckless path, through a gauntlet of grasping jaws and snatching tendrils, until it swam deeper and hid in a clump of swaying weeds.

Mendel had felt the power of the talisman course through him. It had jolted him out of his sleep. Knocked unconscious by the twisting currents, he had lain beneath that old fallen tree too long. But now his feeling of elation at the boy's success was ebbing away. Through the shimmering surface of the great river, he too saw the sky darken and knew it was too soon.

Watching out for Gilgrinders and Burroweels, the wizard flicked his tail and rose as close to the surface as he dared.

A great cloud of death was pouring over the sky above.

He had sensed the destruction of the Scales of Gwendral. And he had somehow felt Dendralon's pain. But never had he imagined the Hedra wizard stooping so low as to unleash the winged dead, the Keresi. They were as big a threat to Dendralon's own kind as to James, Craig or himself.

* * *

James turned the talisman over and over in his hand. It seemed to meld itself into his palm. And its glow cancelled out the deadly crimson that laced the Denthan sky. It was as if...as if the talisman was pumping optimism through his veins.

"Craig?" he pleaded. "Wake up!"

He needed to find Mendel. No, he *would* find Mendel, he decided.

James stood up and felt a rush of power course through him. "I know you are close, Mendel. I can feel it. I will find Dad and save everyone I can, in this world and my own."

The little patch of sky above them still clear, the Yeltans began chanting his name again. Over and over and over...

"James Peck! James Peck! James Peck!"

A fresh breeze filled the clearing and James saw Craig take a long faltering breath.

The story continues in…

CITADEL

Book 2 of *The Peck Chronicles*

Publication: November 2015

Go to **www.stridentpublishing.co.uk** for details.